Cipher

Robert Stohn

Copyright © 2013 Robert Stohn

All rights reserved.

ISBN: 1492202940
ISBN-13: 978-1492202943

CONTENTS

1 1

2 7

3 21

4 37

5 44

6 51

7 60

8 92

9 106

10 118

11 124

12 144

13 151

14 159

15 169

16	**180**
17	**191**
18	**207**
19	**218**
20	**234**
21	**248**
22	**259**
23	**271**
24	**283**
25	**301**
THANK YOU	**306**

1

During the bustling evening rush of passengers hurriedly slipping through the congested Amsterdam Schiphol Airport, a man seated in the corner of one of the many bistros in the terminal area slipped a black USB cipher drive into his laptop and powered the sleek machine on. He watched the glowing screen in front of him as it came to life and carefully scanned the terminal floor from beneath his thick non-prescription lenses. He inconspicuously tapped his finger on the black faux mustache and beard on his face to ensure that they were securely in place. Then, navigating his way across the keyboard with the skill of an artisan, his fingers and hands glided smoothly along as he worked his magic like a master pianist playing his most prized concerto.

Occasionally glancing up to see that everything else in the airport was operating smoothly and efficiently, the man focused his attention on the task at hand. Passengers hurriedly glided across the airport floor under the towering ceiling of white lights slung high above as they made their way to their destinations, all while the man carried out his virtual attack. He appeared just like any other of the thousands of people rushing through or waiting in the airport terminal – a busy traveler using his laptop to check-in remotely to the office. But that's not what he was doing. He watched as the black USB cipher drive whirred to life, and he launched a UNIX systems browser screen. He spent the next few minutes keying in various data and details of his planned targets. He was starting with the Air Traffic Control Systems.

He pounded on the keyboard with lightning fury as the lines of code appeared before him. The white code cast a stark contrast against the black background of the UNIX browser screen. He focused his attention further as he pressed enter, sending the code through the bowels of Cyberspace. He set the timer on his phone for 27 minutes – the time it would take for his hack to take effect. Although nothing changed in that instant when he hit the enter key, he knew what he had just done. He knew what was imminently on the horizon. Air Traffic Control Systems rely on several mainframe databases that communicate information back and forth from airplanes in real time. These databases are responsible for helping to guide all of the airplanes in the sky. They point planes in the right direction, avert crossing flight paths, and help keep people safe. That was all about to change.

The man opened up another UNIX browser window. This time he was after infrastructure in the world's major cities. He spent several more minutes keying in data as he watched the lines of UNIX code spit out results to his commands. He was about to cripple water and power in several major cities throughout the world. He honed in on the destinations he was selecting as his fingers continued to glide across the keys. He knew that it would be catastrophic, but this was only a test. He could bring cities and governments to their knees if he wanted to. He knew that very well. He pressed enter and set another timer for 27 minutes.

The man then opened up a third UNIX browser window. This time, he was after financial institutions. He typed in code with a fury, occasionally glancing at the little black USB cipher box connected to the laptop. He punched in code and it spit back results, line after line. He was working with the obsession of a madman. It was as if he was possessed as his fingers flew across that keyboard. Occasionally, he would glance up and adjust the horn-rimmed glasses. His furious typing didn't even catch a second glance from airport passengers or security that were busy milling about, completely unaware of what was about to happen. He was about to cripple the major financial institutions in the world, and in the process, extract billions of dollars.

The man kept typing away, keying in more details. This one was more complex. He entered several added commands, which included elongated numbered accounts from international banks that were now in his control. The numbers corresponded to the world's most secrecy-shrouded banks. From Panama to Switzerland, he had methodically plotted towards this moment for months, and now he was about to execute his plan. He watched the little black USB cipher drive connected to his laptop whirring, rapidly flashing its orange and green LED lights as it went to work sending crippling ciphers across the Web.

He knew that no one could stop him. He was hopping from one proxy server to the next on the Internet. He was a virtual ghost. No one would even know he existed. He had complete control, and his finger was on the trigger. He knew the power that he held in his hands with that little black cipher drive. He adjusted his tie and breathed in and out slowly. He stared at the UNIX commands being spit back at him from the various windows he had open. 25 minutes and counting. The first window was whirring back commands as it sent the ciphers through the Web in an orchestrated attack on some of the Web's most highly secured databases. He watched carefully as the information was spewed back at him; he watched with intent as his plan carefully unfolded before his very eyes.

He looked around, almost expecting a group of men to appear with assault rifles all pointed in his direction, but they didn't. He really was a ghost. He cracked a half-witted smile as he looked up at the security cameras in the airport terminal. They wouldn't have even known the difference. But the sophisticated hacker had the help of his newly-acquired cipher drive, and with it, he was going to take over the world. As the perspiration built on the side of his face and his fingers continued to fly across the keyboard, he realized that nothing could stop him. No one could stop him. He was virtually invincible, and his only weapon was a little black USB cipher drive. He looked down at the small device connected to his laptop as the lines of UNIX code continued to spew back at an extraordinarily fast rate, and realized the importance of that one tiny device. With that cipher drive, he could do anything. He could conquer the world.

As time wound down, he knew that the moment would soon arrive when all hell would break loose. Cities would fall into complete chaos, the people would riot and loot, and banking systems around the world would virtually collapse. He would be left standing at the helm of one of the largest criminal organizations with the resources to do anything he wanted. He would have the money and the power. The twisted, maniacal thoughts ran through his mind as he slipped the laptop closed. The click of the screen hitting the keyboard put a sense of silent determination into his heart. *This is it,* he thought. *This is finally it.*

2

Jonathan Grace checked his watch – it was quarter past two in the morning when his work phone rang. The continuous digital symphony emanating from the device woke him out of a half-drunken stupor. He felt around his nightstand in the dark as he tried to pull himself together. His nerves were fried and his senses were shot; a 12-hour drinking binge will do that to you. And, even by alcoholics' standards, Jonathan Grace was a force to be reckoned with. He could throw them back with the best of them.

"Hello?" His muffled voice was sure to detract anyone who was calling to harass him at that hour.

"Detective Grace?"

"Who's asking?" No one had called him that in a long time; no one except some of his old clients. His investigative business had all but washed up two years ago, along with his sobriety.

"We need to meet," said the tense voice on the other line. "We have job for you," he added in broken English.

"Who is this?"

"Vinnie. Friend of Joe," he said in more broken English. His thick heavy voice clung to the air like the bad stench of next-day cigarette smoke.

"Joe Cicerone?"

"Si, Si." The voice suddenly sounded much more Italian than it did when he first picked up the phone. Maybe he was starting to finally wake up.

"Okay. When?" Jonathan asked.

"Tomorrow. Noon."

"Where?"

"Bethesda Fountain. Central Park."

"Okay, I'll be there," Jonathan hummed back. He was still trying to get his bearings.

"See you," said the voice on the other end. And with that, the phone clicked. Jonathan looked at it and scratched his head. He hadn't taken a job in ages and his thinning roster of clients was a product of his increased efficiency in boozing. He knew he had to pull himself together. He rummaged around in his nightstand drawer looking for something to write on. He remembered placing a notepad in there somewhere, and began tossing out socks and underwear until he located a pad and pen. He scribbled down some notes and tried to jar his memory. His head was still throbbing but he had to try to do it while it was fresh in his head.

Don Joe Cicerone – Cicerone Family Head – Little Italy
12:00pm Central Park – Bethesda Fountain

The next day, Jonathan could feel the effects of his hangover. He could feel his throbbing head and his dry mouth as soon as he opened his eyes. He was paying the price for his poor decisions, but that was always the case. He seemed to always be paying the price; at least that's how the past two years had been. He tried to shake it off. He thought back to the phone call and tried to pull himself together. He knew he needed to nurse his hangover, and he did it like any other professional drinker would – by pouring himself another drink. He cracked opened the near-desolate fridge and scanned the shelves – vodka, tomato juice, Worcester sauce – he had found breakfast. He carefully blended a morning meal – a Bloody Mary it was. He plopped in a handful of ice cubes, dashed it with some salt, and stirred it with his pinky finger. Perfection.

He gulped it down hard. The concoction hit just the right spot, but it was still to early for him to be up. It had been ages since he had woken up early to meet a client. Early by his standards meant anything before noon. He had become accustomed to the *late wake* as he would describe it to the few close friends he still had left. He checked his watch – only an hour to go before the meeting. He thought about Don Cicerone and the meeting as he surveyed the atomic bomb that had gone off in his apartment. He scanned the empty pizza boxes, empty cans of beer, and the kitchen sink full of dishes as he thought about the type of jobs he had been given in the past from the Cicerone family. He was always tasked with digging up the dirt that no one else could find. That's why they came to him – he used to be the best in the business.

Looking around his own apartment, he realized that he sure didn't feel confident anymore. In fact, he was completely out of sync with reality. He was a rusty nail in an old beat-up toolbox. After throwing back the bottle for the past couple of years, his thinning roster of clients was barely helping edge him by in life. But he kept those few clients because that's what kept him going; that's what kept the pleasure-train rolling. Without them, the river would dry up, and Jonathan would actually have to man up. He didn't want to face the music. He wasn't ready for that. He wasn't remotely ready for anything like that. No rehab. No sobriety. Nothing. All he wanted to do was get by, and that's just what he had been doing.

He hit the streets to a sweltering gust of heat outside his Brooklyn apartment. New York City was ablaze with a heat wave. Not just any old heat wave. The intense humidity seemed to make the air boil over with discomfort. It was hot and muggy out. Jonathan dressed the part in an effort to keep cool – beige khakis, a white polo tee was in order for the day, and a silver set of aviators to keep the glaring sun away from his very hungover state-of-mind. He would have preferred to be indoors where he could feel the cool breeze of the air conditioning on his face, but he had no choice. Vinnie was waiting, and it was for Don Cicerone. He thought about the Italian mob boss, and what he could have possibly wanted him to help him with this time. He had been one of his best clients, but after a year of not hearing from him, he thought he had been all but forgotten.

Jonathan tried to fan his face as he dropped down below Church Street and into the depths of the New York subway system. The hot street-level air gave way to a subterranean inferno down below. It was midday, so the Brooklyn subway platform was dotted with only a few passengers. Most people were at work at that hour. As the Five train approached, the hot gust of wind made it almost unbearable to be down there. Coupled with the hangover he was still trying to nurse, the blast of hot air made him feel lightheaded. He walked onto the air-conditioned subway car and was welcomed gust of cool air. He could relax. He sat down, eyed the passengers, and tried to pull himself together.

He pulled out his phone and leafed through his messages. He was just killing time, but he couldn't help but think about Don Cicerone again. The fear of working for one of the most repudiated mob families in New York was tempered by his need for cash. Jonathan was going broke, and he needed to do something fast. He had been burning through whatever savings he had ever since he started binge drinking again. The subway stopped at Dyre Avenue in lower Manhattan, and he hoofed it to transfer to the C Train. He still had about thirty minutes to go as he headed towards the Fulton Street transfer.

When he finally arrived at the 72nd Street stop, he sensed some pent-up anxiety. Why had they called him after so long? What was so important that it couldn't be discussed over the phone? Why the call at 2 o'clock in the morning? The secrecy that shrouded the job was eating at him. As he hoofed his way in the sweltering heat towards Bethesda Fountain in Central Park, he rubbed the sweat off his forehead. The unbearable weather made it difficult to be outside. The 100-plus degree heat made even the least strenuous activity difficult. Although the brisk walk was just a short trek through the park, Jonathan was drenched in sweat.

When he reached the fountain, he was out of breath. He wasn't sure who he would be looking for because he didn't know what Vinnie looked like, so he sat down on the fountain's edge. The cool mist from the water made being by the fountain more bearable. He faced the terrace just to the south of the fountain and wished he were standing under the protection of it. He looked around at all the people who had filled the park that day – it was late summer and tourism in New York City was at its peak. He looked around to survey the other park goers and checked his watch – 11:58am. He had made it with only minutes to spare. But where was Vinnie?

Jonathan checked his watch again – 12:05pm. They were late. Maybe he just wasn't noticeable enough. Maybe he needed to stand up so that they would be able to spot him. It wasn't the first time he was meeting someone blind on the spot, meaning he didn't know who he was looking for. But, they usually knew to look for him, and he figured today wouldn't have been any different. He checked his watch one final time – 12:08pm. They were really late. Jonathan looked around one more time before standing up to stretch when a man selling balloons approached him. He handed him a blue balloon.

"This is for you," said the man with balloons.

"No thank you, I really don't want a balloon," he barked back.

"Yes you do. You want this balloon. Take this balloon and walk up through the terrace and onto the other side. Wait there for a black town car to pick you up." The man with the balloons walked off just as quickly as he had appeared. He left headed north through the park, opposite the direction Jonathan was supposed to go.

He didn't wait around any longer. He took the balloon, walked through the ornately decorated Bethesda Terrace, and quickly ascended the steps on the other side towards Terrace Drive. When he got there, he stood and waited with his blue balloon. *I feel like a fool holding this thing.* He watched as car after car drove by, mostly taxis, until a black town car stopped in front of him. The driver rolled the window down.

"Get in," said the beefy man with a triple chin.

Jonathan hopped in the back seat, and looked at the overweight thug in the driver's seat. He had on all black. A black suit jacket, black dress shirt, black tie, and black pants. He looked like he was on his way to a funeral. His overtly Italian accent meant that he was most likely new to the states.

"Hi, so where to?" Jonathan tried to play friendly. He tried to be nice.

"Uptown," he said in his very thick accent.

Jonathan got the point that the man was either in no mood to talk, or didn't really have the vocabulary to strike up a conversation. So, he just sat in the car, still nursing his hangover, and watched the scenery go by as they made their way uptown. The car veered out of Central Park heading north on Broadway. They made their way west towards the Hudson River when they hit 96th Street. He still wasn't sure where they were going, but Jonathan knew enough to keep his mouth shut. He looked at the glum driver every now and then who had a proclivity to keep his hand on the horn for a few seconds too long each time he thought another car was in his way. A barrage of Italian spoken excessively fast and foul would follow each incident.

They finally arrived at their destination at the Riverside Clay Tennis Association. It wasn't the strangest place they could go, but it certainly was out of character for old Don Cicerone. They got out of the car and walked towards a grassy tree-lined area by the water.

"Follow me," he said again in that thick accent.

Jonathan followed the 400-plus pound Italian thug as he led him through the serene park to a tree where two men stood amidst people lying in the sun trying to soak up the rays and catch a tan.

"Thanks for coming," said Don Cicerone.

"Interesting place to meet. It's been a long time," replied Jonathan.

"You look like shit."

Jonathan ran his hand through his hair. "It was long night," he said meekly.

"You look worse than shit, actually. What happened to you?"

Jonathan wasn't sure how to answer that question. *What happened to me? Life happened to me.* He had been battered and bruised by a string of experiences that left him emotionally and financially broke, battered, and bruised. "It's been a bad year… a bad couple of years"

"Well, you look like a schmuck. Clean yourself up, kid. You've got some work to do."

"What's the job?" Jonathan asked.

"The most important job of your life."

Jonathan's interest was peaked. "Yeah?"

"I need you to locate something for me."

"Got a name?"

"It's not a person. It's a USB drive. A USB *cipher* drive. A small four-inch by one-inch square." As the Don spoke, Jonathan surveyed the sweaty monstrosity in front of him. It was like speaking to two people at once.

"You want me to find a hard drive for you?"

"Not just any drive, you idiot," he said. He slicked his jet-black hair back with one of his meaty hands. Jonathan noticed the excessive gold rings and bracelets on his hand that jingled as he moved it. "This drive has something very valuable to me on it. Let's just say it's a special kind of drive. Anyways, I need you to find it."

"Okay."

"Just okay? This is important. Don't you have any questions for me?"

Jonathan Grace wasn't used to locating a thing; he specialized in finding people. He used to be one of the best detectives out there, but this task was different. He stared at

Don Cicerone as he stood there before him; his mane of chest hairs protruding from the black V-neck shirt he had on.

"What's on the drive?"

"Something very important to me," barked Don Cicerone. He started getting agitated with Jonathan.

"Okay, but look…"

"No look kid. This is very important. That drive belongs to me and I need it back. I need it back badly. It was taken from me and if I don't get it back someone is going to pay. If you can't do the job, I'll find someone else who can. Just say the word, kid."

"Okay. I'll find your drive, Don Cicerone."

"You better, kid." He handed Jonathan a yellow envelope stuffed with one hundred dollar bills. "Here's 100k upfront. Should cover all your travel costs along with a sizable retainer."

Jonathan stared at the envelope, then leafed through the cash inside. It was more money than he had seen in over a year. "Thanks."

"One million dollars when you return the cipher drive to me, safe and sound, along with the person who had it."

Jonathan's mouth just about dropped to the floor. He tried not to show how impressed he was, and worried that the job was over his head, but he didn't dare say that. He looked down at the black Italian loafers Don Cicerone was wearing and got lost in a train of thought for a moment.

"Hey kid, you with me?" said Don Cicerone in an effort to ensure that he was heard.

"Yes. Yeah… I mean…it's a deal."

"Good. All of the info is on this." Don Cicerone handed him a silver USB stick. "If you have any questions, you can always call Vinnie over here," he said, nodding to the driver who picked him up.

"Okay, got it."

"And, kid."

"Yeah?"

"You screw me over and it's two bullets to the head."

"I'll find it. I assure you that I'll find it." Jonathan sounded much more confident this time around. He had a renewed sense of spirit. This was his big chance – his big opportunity to pull his life back together and get back to some semblance of normalcy. He couldn't screw this up. *He wouldn't screw this up.*

"That's more like it. I expect you to check in with me often. At least a couple times a week. Let me know your progress. I wanna know where we're at with this at all times. That drive… that *muthafuckin'* cipher drive… is the most important thing in my life. It's more important than my wife and my unborn children. You understand me?"

"Perfectly. Loud and clear, Don Cicerone. Sir."

"Good. Vinnie, give the kid a lift back to the park."

"Done."

3

Jonathan rubbed his eyes and stared at the computer screen in front of him, then at the silver USB stick in his hands. The large yellow envelope of cash lay on his desk next to him. He eyed it with suspicion. He knew what kind of trouble that money could bring to his life. He knew just what type of hijinks he could get into if he allowed himself. But he knew he couldn't. This was Don Cicerone, and he couldn't mess around. He had to get started on the job and get him back the information he was looking for. He knew he couldn't let him down.

The thin silver USB stick felt so innocent in his hands.

He imagined it would be quite like the black USB cipher drive he was after, except that one seemed a bit more ominous. That black USB cipher drive had something on it worth a lot of money to a very powerful man. Jonathan could only imagine what it was, and to what extent the repudiated mob boss would be willing to go to in order to get it back. He felt the brushed aluminum of the silver USB stick as he slipped it into his sleek laptop. An orange light blinked rapidly as the data was accessed and a folder was launched containing three files: one picture, a voice recording, and a document.

He clicked on the first file – the image. It opened up to reveal a black and white photo of a tall blonde woman taken with what appeared to be a high-zoom lens. Dr. Jennifer M. Cobalt was the name at bottom of the photo. He studied the image carefully. He studied the look on the woman's face. Her delicate white complexion and high cheekbones drew him in. The woman in the photo fascinated him. Who was she? What was her story? He carefully clicked the mouse, moving the image to the side as he opened the next file, a PDF document. It was some sort of map of Istanbul. But it wasn't an ordinary map. It was overlaid with coordinates and other details. In the bottom corner of the map there was a paragraph about 2048-bit encryption keys. He reviewed the map for a few moments before pushing it aside and clicking on the last file – the audio file. He launched it and listened to it play. It was the sound of woman's voice recording her findings.

Woman's voice: August 4th, 2:14pm – 1024-bit RSA keys no longer have the protection value they once did. This loaded cipher drive can crack the standard 1024-bit RSA key in just less than 27 minutes, far quicker than the standard 11-month time frame required for cracking a 1024-bit RSA key. I've created the cipher using a new string of algorithms that exponentially increases the speed of brute force crack. This technology, if found in the wrong hands, could be used to hack government, banking, and infrastructure on the Internet like never before. There would be no stopping anyone who got their hands on it.

Man's voice: What will you do with the technology now that you've achieved your goal of creating a sub one-hour cracking cipher for the standard 1024-bit RSA key?

Woman's voice: My team is now working on the holy grail of all cracking ciphers: the 2048-bit RSA key crack. These RSA keys are rare in the field of cryptology, but as Moore's law of computing technology doubles every 18 to 24 months, it won't be long until 2048-bit RSA keys become the standard. I won't rest until we reach that goal.

Man's voice: And you think it's possible to create that kind of crack? The complexities are incredulous for cracking something like that.

Woman's voice: Yes, it's 2 to the nth power with 2048 being n in this case. Yes, we're well aware of the complexities. But this is the task. This is what we've been commissioned to complete.

The audio recording stopped, and Jonathan Grace sat back in his chair, still staring at the audio recording on his laptop screen. *God, this is going to change the world. With this technology, he can break into anything. Any bank, any government institution, any state infrastructure; literally, anything.* He now realized why the pay was so high and why Don Cicerone was willing to do just about anything to get that cipher drive back. What were his intentions with it? It couldn't be anything good, but who was he to judge? The Don was a paying client and the only person keeping him solvent right now.

He opened the yellow envelope again and leafed through the five twenty-thousand-dollar stacks of hundred-dollar bills. He knew what he needed to do now. He knew what the job entailed, but where would he start? Where was he going to go from here? He stared at his laptop for a few minutes. He knew it wasn't going to be easy. He knew he had to start out by doing research. He needed to find out everything he could possibly know about this woman and the technology she held in her hands. He needed to find out where she was, how she spent her day, and somehow get close enough to her to grab the drive. He knew it wasn't going to be easy. He knew that he had his work cut out for him.

*****

After a long, full day of travel, Jonathan found himself in the passenger terminal at the Istanbul Ataturk Airport. He looked around, studying the passengers that were busy making their way to their destinations, rushing to connecting flights, or leaving the airport to head home. All of them were completely oblivious to the technological doomsday device that was floating around somewhere nearby. They were completely unaware of the power that a small four by one piece of computer hardware could have on the global economy. A complete shutdown and draining of money from financial systems or a complete rewiring of city and state infrastructure through coordinated hacks were just a couple of the catastrophes that the device could be used to perpetrate.

You're going to make one million dollars, Jonathan. One million dollars. It was more money than he had ever seen and the allure of the profit and his fear of the client drove him to push through any mental roadblocks he may have had of doing the job. He was going to find the woman and he was going to find the hardware. But why him? Why had Don Cicerone picked him to do the job? Jonathan knew that he was capable, but it was clear that he had been falling apart in recent years. He must have seen that when they met in the park. He must have known that, but still decided to go with him for the job. He felt honored that they chose him, but he did have a great rapport with them in the past. In the past, when they needed something, he always came through. He could always find the man or the woman they were looking for, without fail.

He thought about Don Cicerone and what would happen to him if he failed as he waited in the taxi line outside the airport terminal. The air was hot, and the New York heat wave was seemingly mirrored in Istanbul. He couldn't get away from the heat. He couldn't escape it even if he tried. It was the middle of summer and it felt exactly like it. He was in unfamiliar territory but that didn't distract him from what he knew needed to be done. Scanning the busy terminal, Jonathan made his way outside to hail a taxi and get to the city center. He had brushed up on Turkish phrases on the flight over, and tried to recite them in his mind. The language wasn't easy to pick up, and he knew it was going to take some work to get acclimated.

"Merhaba," said the taxi driver as he climbed in.

"Merhaba," said Jonathan back. That was an easy one. It meant 'hello'. "Do you speak English?"

"Yes. Little," replied the cabbie in broken English. "Where will you go?"

"Besiktas?" said Jonathan, naming the area of the city where the hotel was located.

"Oh, okay. You mean Beşiktaş? To a hotel?"

"Yes. The Le Hotel."

"Okay, no problem. Where are from?" His English was bad but it was better than him trying to communicate with him in Turkish. He wasn't at a conversational level just yet.

"New York City."

"Oh, New York City. I love New York," he said, laughing to himself. "Very big city. Like Istanbul."

"Yes, very big city," Jonathan replied.

"You come vacation in Istanbul?"

Jonathan looked at the man through the rearview mirror. He seemed like an innocent, hardworking man. The thick dark mustache made it difficult to see his mouth.

"No, for work."

"Oh, okay. For what kind of work you do?"

"I'm an investigator. Like a detective." Jonathan didn't mind the conversation, but he was enjoying taking in the sights and the sounds of the new city. It was the first time he had ever been to Istanbul and he enjoyed the change of scenery. Stuck in a rut, the doldrums of living in New York wore on him. Although it was a city full of opportunity, his opportunity had been in the dirt for a while now, and he was happy to finally get a good break.

"You are police?" The taxi driver looked at Jonathan now with suspect through the rearview mirror, and he didn't seem like the type of person who liked police.

"No. No. Not police. Private investigator for private clients."

"Oh. Okay. Police here no good. I don't like."

"I understand. Not many people do like the police when they have to deal with them. The taxi drivers in New York complain about the police too." Jonathan lied. He wanted to get the cabbie back on his side again.

"Yes. Police sometimes very bad. They take money. They steal."

"Really?" Jonathan hadn't realized that corruption was that apparent in a city like Istanbul, but it didn't shock him. It didn't shock him that there were people in power gaming the system. It was probably just more apparent in a city like

Istanbul, but he knew that kind of corruption existed everywhere. Some countries were just better at hiding it than others. If you took a country like the United States, you might not visibly see the corruption, but it still existed. Jonathan knew all too well just how much it existed. He had been tasked with helping to uncover some of that corruption in his early days as a detective working in the city. But that was in the past. He didn't want to go backwards.

"Evet. Really."

He had recalled the word *evet*, which meant yes in Turkish. He looked at the working-class man through the rear view mirror again, then at the ancient city as they drove over a spectacular bridge across the Bosporus, separating the Asian side of Turkey from the European side. The shimmering city's mosques glittered in the distance as they made their way over the large suspension bridge. Jonathan couldn't recall seeing anything so beautiful in such a long time.

The city sparkled along the water and he was hit with a rush of excitement and exhilaration. He knew he had work to do, but just breathing in the air of the ancient city made him feel more alive. He was no longer confined to the bowels of New York City; he was really living life. This was it. This was what it was all about. He wrapped both arms around his backpack as if it were a little child on his lap. That backpack contained virtually his entire life at that moment.

On the last stretch of road before they reached the hotel, Jonathan marveled at the sparkling sea. He looked at the dichotomy in women, some wearing burkas, some without, and realized how far away from home he really was. But he didn't mind. He didn't mind being far away form home because of the rich historical beauty that he found himself immersed in. The city made him feel alive again. It made him feel like a person. He had a purpose and a meaning to his life. He didn't have to drift away in some dingy apartment in Brooklyn; he could live again doing what he knew how to do best. As long as he didn't mess up the opportunity, there would surely be more to come for him.

When he finally reached the hotel, he thanked the taxi driver. He took one last moment to look at him as he shook his hand before walking into the hotel with his bag. The cobblestone and historical exterior provided a stark contrast to the sleek and modern interior of the Le Hotel in Istanbul. The blacks and reds accented the space with brilliant pops of color that brought the hotel to life. The contemporary furniture with its clean lines gave way to rich, brilliantly colored finishes throughout the space. While checking in, he marveled at the beauty of the place for a moment and felt pleased with himself for having found that gem.

He took a moment to gather himself as he walked into the stylish guest room that had all the comforts of home. He stepped out onto the small terrace and sat there for a few moments collecting his thoughts. The seven-hour time difference ahead from New York was going to catch up with him at some point, but he still had energy from the sleep he caught on the flight. He walked back into the room and decided to setup his laptop and get to work. He had to find Dr. Cobalt and get the black USB cipher drive. He stared at the PDF map on his screen for a few moments. He studied the coordinates and other detailed information on the map, then minimized it on his screen. He opened up another browser, and this time decided to do a Google search for information on Dr. Cobalt to see what he could come up with.

Jonathan used to be a pro at surfing the Web. Before he allowed the drinking to get in the way, he was one of the most proficient investigators that there was. He was trying to find that in him again. He wanted so badly to succeed, because it also meant getting his life back together. That money meant a sense of normalcy; a life where he didn't have to take dead-end jobs that paid next to nothing. It was the chance of a lifetime and he was hoping and praying that he wouldn't screw it up. As he stood there staring at the Web browser, he keyed in information in a variety of different formats. He started with the search "Dr. Jennifer M. Cobalt," in the search field on Google to see what he would come up with. Of course, there were loads of links with a variety of news articles.

He clicked on the first news link in the search, which led him to a popular news piece from the New York Times about the researcher. He read the information to find out more about her work and research. She had a PhD in mathematical physics from Harvard University, and she had been hailed as the leading mind in mathematics. He read a part of the article that discussed the doctor and her work.

Turkish born, Dr. Jennifer M. Cobalt, a fellow at Harvard University, is blazing a trail in applied mathematics and advanced cryptology algorithms. Her research has been hailed as revolutionary and ground breaking.

He looked at the documents on the silver USB stick that were given to him by Don Cicerone again. He reviewed the information to see if he could find a phone number or an address, something that would lead him closer to the esteemed Doctor and her storied creation. Towards the end of his search, he located an address on Bağdat Avenue in Istanbul and a phone number. Fearing that time had rendered the information outdated, he decided that he would start there anyway. She wouldn't be that difficult to locate; he knew that. But, locating the black USB cipher drive might prove to be much more difficult. That was the goal, anyhow – to locate the cipher drive. He picked up his cell phone and decided to call, and a woman answered the phone.

"Evet?" said the voice on the other end in Turkish.

"Hello? Hi, can I speak with Dr. Cobalt please?"

There was a pause on the other end of the line, as if almost expecting the phone call. "Who is this?"

"My name is Jonathan Grace."

"I'm sorry, but Ms. Cobalt is not here," said the woman in near-perfect English.

"Can I leave a message with her?"

Another pause on the other end of the line. "What is this about please?" she asked politely.

"I have something very important that I need to discuss with her. I can only discuss it with her. Can you please have her call me? I need to speak to her right away."

"Yes, okay. I will have her call you. She will be back this evening."

Jonathan gave the woman his phone number and hung up. After the conversation, he felt uneasy, almost as if it seemed to good to be true. Would she be that easy to reach? Would she be that simple to find? Maybe it was some sort of test. He looked around the room and thought about it for a few moments. He ran the ideas through his mind. He didn't know where he was supposed to go from there. He felt lost. He couldn't do much until he heard from the woman.

Wait, what about the map? What about the coordinates on the map? Jonathan had a flash of an idea suddenly. It hit him like a pile of bricks being suddenly dropped on his head. The coordinates must lead somewhere. Maybe he would follow the coordinates. He looked at the map again. He analyzed it with great detail. He couldn't tell if the hand-written coordinates were GPS coordinates. They looked similar to GPS coordinates with a latitude and longitude, but they had too many digits. It almost seemed like it was a cipher in and of itself. He looked at them for twenty minutes, trying to understand what they meant. He wrote and rewrote the numbers out on a notepad in various different formats, but to no avail.

He was growing increasingly weary by the moment as the jet lag started to kick in. The coordinates weren't making sense to him. What could they be pointing to? What was the overlay on the map referring to? Was it directions to somewhere? Was he supposed to follow the coordinates to find the black USB cipher drive? That couldn't have been it; it couldn't have been that easy. That didn't make sense. He was only hours away from connecting with Dr. Cobalt, and if she didn't have the black USB cipher drive, then she had to know who did. She had to be the one that could divulge that information to him. If she couldn't, he didn't know what he was going to do. He wasn't sure in what direction it would lead him, but he knew he had to follow.

His mind was racing at a million miles a minute. He opened up the hotel safe and stashed a large portion of his cash in there along with his other valuables. He decided he needed some rest. He needed to lie down if he was going to be at all productive. The seven-hour time difference was starting to catch up even though he had caught some sleep on the plane; the full day of travel was finally starting to wear on him. His initial burst of energy had all but worn off. He was tired. And, as his eyelids sagged, he stared at the bed that looked so comfortable. He stared at it for just long enough when he decided he was tired enough to sleep. *Just a few hours of shuteye. That's all I need. Just a few hours of shuteye.*

4

Major chaos today in cities across the world when water and power failed in 7 major metropolitan areas including London, New York, Los Angeles, Miami, Paris, Hong Kong, and Sydney. The power outages were widespread and it's been suspected that the attack was a coordinated effort against the major water and power distributors. All efforts are being taken to restore power in cities across the world where hundreds of millions have been affected. Air traffic and control in several major cities have also reported problems, with planes experiencing major diversions in flight paths and interruptions in communications. And, financial markets have taken a big hit today as the major indices around the world plunged as hackers gained access to institutions across the globe. It's been estimated that billions of dollars have gone missing. The FBI, NSA, CIA, Interpol, MI6, and other international agencies are still searching for clues but all are saying that this is the most sophisticated coordinated attack they have ever seen. Stay tuned for the full story.

In a war room located deep beneath the bowels of the White House in Washington, D.C., the President of the United States assembled his top secretaries. Present in the room were the Directors of the FBI, CIA, NSA, Joint Chiefs of Staff, the Secretary of Defense, and the Vice President. The President sat at the head of the table silently, looking at each of his trusted members of the government. The air in the room was tense; you could slice the tension with a knife. The President, with his hands folded on the table in front of him, had a silent look of determination on his face.

"How could we let this happen? How did we not know about this?" asked the President, looking at each member one by one as he said the words slowly. He turned to look at his intelligence officers and paused at the Director of the NSA, Peter Edwards.

"President Meyers, sir, this blindsided us." He looked the President squarely in the eyes. "It's the most sophisticated attack we've seen, and the coordination of all these diverse targets is extraordinary."

"Who's pulling these strings?" asked the President. "I don't want to hear about how sophisticated this operation has been. That's already very clear. Just look at the news right now. The world is plunging into chaos and there's sure to be more to follow. What are our people doing right now to contain this?" This time he turned to look at the FBI Director Ryan Shilling. "Ryan? What are your thoughts?"

"Sir, we're pulling out all stops on this one. We have some ideas of who's pulling these strings. On the screen in front of you is Boris Medviek, former Russian KGB, and Special Operations Soldier. We think he may have something to do with this. Our chatter is pointing towards the Russians."

"What do we know about Medviek? How do we know for certain that he's behind this?" asked the President again, this time looking at his Director of the CIA, Michael Waterman.

"Sir, we have preliminary knowledge of the possibility of his involvement, but we're still attempting to confirm certain information. We are unclear of his whereabouts now, but we are working with our agents on the ground to get a pinpoint on him. Sources have him in either Istanbul or Amsterdam, and he may also be back in Moscow. He knows how to evade tracking, but we'll get a location on him soon."

"Look," said the President, "I know that we can all say what we should have or could have done to avoid this crisis, but it's here and we need to deal with it. I need to know that our best people are on this. We can't let this situation balloon out of control. If this Medviek is coordinating these attacks, then we need to find him and put a stop to this. God knows the potential extent of further damage."

"Sir, I agree," said the Chairman of the Joint Chiefs of Staff, Donald Elmington. "And this information doesn't leave these four walls. We cannot allow the American public to know what caused this. We can't allow fear to grow in the hearts of people. It would cause sheer panic and chaos. But, if this Medviek decides to further these attacks and goes after energy facilities or atomic generators, we could be in grave trouble."

"Don, we can't allow that to happen. We can't allow the lives of millions of people to be in the balance here. We have to do something to stop this. And we have to do it right away. We need a plan, people. I want a status report tonight at twenty-one hundred hours. Is that clear?" said the President.

The President looked at the members in attendance of the meeting. The air was just as tense as when the meeting began, if not more. The bunker-like war room had set the tone for what was to come.

"Mr. President. If I may say something, sir," said Secretary of Defense Palmer.

"Yes, go ahead, Steven," said the President.

"I think we need to prepare for a doomsday situation here. I don't think we need to panic the American people, but we need to be prepared. My staff has done some estimates of the damage that could be caused if nuclear and weapons facilities are hit, and it could be catastrophic. Mr. President, this could be thousands of times worse than 9/11. This trumps all of our worries in the Middle East...and the secular extremists."

The Secretary of Defense pressed a button on his tablet screen and sent the imagery of the nuclear facilities that could be targeted around the world. The images of destruction and devastation showed a huge radius of potential global terror. "You'll see in the image above, the destruction could be catastrophic. This Medviek was able to hit three diverse systems all at once. We can only imagine what else he can do," added Secretary of Defense Palmer.

The room grew quiet. Not another word was said. The President looked from one set of eyes to the next in the room. He knew the severity of the situation. He knew what could happen if they allowed this thing to get out of control. He looked at his Chairman of the Joint Chiefs of Staff, Elmington.

"Don, what do you think? Do we go to the American people with this? If we do, we could cause complete panic. If we don't, and something goes very wrong, we could be risking a lot more by holding this from them."

"I've been thinking about that Mr. President. But, I think that at this time, until we can accurately assess the real threat to the American people, that we keep this under wraps. I think we need to employ all assets in the field to locate Medviek. Once we've got some more intelligence on him and the situation, then we should reassess."

The President looked pleased with his view. He looked around the room at the others seated at the table.

"Everyone in agreement with that?" asked the President.

They all agreed in unison, and the President excused them. He asked everyone to leave, aside from the Vice President, Ron Jenkins.

"Ronnie, we're in deep shit with this," said the President.

"I know we are. I know we are."

"What's your take on this?"

"I think Don had a good point about not going to the public with it until we're absolutely certain of the real threat, but we need to make some moves here. Each moment we lose is a moment we can't spare."

"I agree. We need to get a location on Medviek. I want you to push everyone involved as much as you can. This is top priority now. This supersedes everything else we've got going on. If this Medviek can access systems like this, then there's no stopping him."

"Okay, I'll get on it, Mr. President," said the Vice President.

"Okay. Good. Keep me updated."

"Okay. Sounds good, Mr. President."

5

The white and chrome finish of the 245-foot luxury superyacht glistened under the hot summer sun. Anchored just a few hundred feet off the shores of Portofino, Italy, the sleek, stylish lines of the superyacht elegantly bent along the exotic hull of the modern floating mansion. Boris Medviek looked out onto the crystal blue ocean waters and cloudless blue skies from the rear upper deck. He admired the view of the vividly colored buildings that hung almost dangerously along the cliffs of the famed Cinque Terre city. The brightly colored reds, yellows, and oranges of the buildings gently mixed with the blues of the ocean and skies to cast a painted masterpiece that could have been hung in any world-class art gallery.

Boris's two most trusted lieutenants sat at a teakwood table with five Eastern European supermodels. The Russian, Ukrainian, and Czech girls smiled and nodded, bobbing their head to the electronic music playing in the background as they sipped champagne. Boris smiled and raised his glass to his comrades. He looked on towards the shores of the Portofino beach through dark sunglasses and reveled in his own accomplishments. He had done it. He had effectively used the cipher drive to wreak havoc and, in effect, capture billions of dollars. It was easy. Almost too easy.

"Like taking candy from babies," he said in near-perfect English but with a Russian accent. He raised his glass further, and motioned for one of the deckhands to quickly top off all of the champagne. The girls raised their glasses too but they had no idea what they were toasting to.

"To more success," said Dmitry, his most trusted lieutenant and brother, who sat at the table with the girls. They clinked their glasses and all drank the champagne. Boris finished his first with a toss straight down the throat like a true Russian. He smiled and called for more.

Off in the distance, the silent rumble of a helicopter

cut through the summer air as it neared. They could all hear the sound, as the chopper got closer until it finally appeared around the inlet of Portofino. The black EC155 helicopter hovered directly over the superyacht as it slowly descended onto the landing pad on the ship's upper deck, in plain sight of all the onlookers.

"He's here," said Boris.

"Yes," said Dmitry. "Girls, downstairs. Now!" He yelled at them to scram as the chopper killed its engine and the blades made their final whining noise. They came to an abrupt stop and the door opened.

Standing up from their chairs, Boris alone walked towards the chopper as a small entourage of Saudis disembarked. "Sheik Abdullah. So good to see you, your highness," said Boris.

"Thank you for having me," said the middle-aged Saudi Sheik. They did a non-contact kiss in the air towards both cheeks as they shook hands. Boris did it as a sign of respect.

"Thank you for coming. Shall we have a seat?" he asked, pointing towards the seating area already setup on the upper deck. Boris snapped his fingers and the table was quickly cleared of all alcohol out of respect for the Saudi. Then, just as quickly as the alcohol had disappeared, a variety of fresh fruits, juices, breads, croissants, and jams found their way to the table.

"Yes, thank you," said the Sheik, taking a seat at the oversized round table. "Good of you to invite me." The Sheik's armed bodyguards took positions at the rear corners of the ship, flanking the wealthy Saudi.

"Please, can I offer you some coffee, tea, or juice?"

"Tea. The Sheik likes tea," said one of the men who had arrived as part of the Sheik's entourage.

"I'm sorry. Excuse me. This is Salem. He is my most trusted advisor." The Sheik looked at Boris and Dmitry as he was speaking. A deckhand appeared and poured tea for the Sheik and Salem.

"Of course," replied Boris. "Anything you want here is yours. Just name it," cooed Dmitry with a smile on his face.

"You know what I really want. You know the reason that I'm here," said the Sheik.

"Yes, of course. And it won't be a problem," said Boris slyly.

"Are you sure?"

"Yes, I'm sure."

"How can you be certain?" The Sheik looked at Boris with intent. He knew what he was asking for, and Boris knew that he could give it to him.

"Have you read the headlines in the news lately? Power

outages in New York, London, and Hong Kong?"

"Yes, of course," said the Sheik.

Boris smiled.

"This was you?"

"Yes. And have you heard of the Air Traffic Control headaches lately in several cities across the world? How about the financial collapse of intraday trading on many indices across the globe?"

"Yes, of course. I have. All of them."

Boris smiled again.

"This was you?" asked the Sheik.

"Yes. It was a coordinated attack. They did not suspect it coming."

"And what if they are more prepared the next time you attempt this type of attack? How will you get me the information that I am seeking?"

"They cannot safeguard anything. I can provide you the information that you're after, but it won't come cheap." Boris looked at the Sheik squarely in the eyes and spoke with a great deal of intent. He was more than confident he could extract the information that he needed. He could provide him with what he was looking for.

"Okay, we'll see. How much?"

"One billion US dollars for each 1000 names of agents."

"That is a very steep price to pay," said the Sheik.

"Yes, but you have very few alternatives. I will make sure you get those names." Boris knew what he had to do. It was going to be one of the most daring heists that would be pulled off this century. The real names and identities of the field agents for the CIA, FBI, MI6, and Interpol stationed around the world would be the most lethal information that could be extracted from the world's governments.

"Okay. I will trust that you can provide me with this information," said the Sheik as he sipped his tea from the white porcelain cup.

"I assure you that I can provide you with that information. I will require a 10% deposit of the funds now, and the rest on delivery."

"I will require all of the names on the list," said the Sheik. "And 10% will not be a problem."

Boris did the math in his head. Roughly, 3400 names would be 3.4 billion US dollars. He gave a quick glance to Dmitry, and then smiled at the Sheik.

"I will be more than happy to oblige. I'll need three weeks to deliver the data. And I will only deliver it in person."

"I would expect nothing different," said the Sheik.

"Please, shall we have some fun now?" Boris snapped his fingers to call the girls back to the deck now that their work was complete. They happily clamored back upstairs to join the group.

6

At a busy café on Bağdat Avenue in Istanbul, Turkey, Jonathan Grace sat with Dr. Jennifer Cobalt. The street was packed with people. It was a weekend, and the roads and walkways were filled with pedestrians out for an evening stroll, window-shopping, or on their way to get a bite to eat. The rich aromas of lamb and chicken, along with Mediterranean spices, filled the air. Jonathan sat soaking it all in. Everything about the place was different. He looked at the people as they passed by and wondered what each of their stories was.

"Thank you for the taking the time to meet with me, Dr.

Cobalt," he said.

"I don't have much time, and please just call me Jennifer," she replied. "What was so important that you wanted to speak to me about that you had to fly 5,000 miles to meet with me in person?"

"It's about your research," Jonathan said as he took a sip of the tea in the thin, slender, curved transparent glass.

"The advanced algorithms?" she asked, taking off her slender brown frames and placing them on the table. She sat back and crossed her legs and her arms. She was closing herself off to the world.

"Yes."

"Who sent you?"

"I can't discuss that with you," said Jonathan, taking another sip of the tea.

"I knew I should have never gotten involved with that project. My friends and colleagues all warned me, but I didn't listen."

"Warned you about what?"

"The project. It got out of hand. It got very out of hand," she said silently as if someone was going to overhear their conversation.

"I'm afraid I still don't follow. I need some background information. Can you tell me more about it? I don't have that much information to go on." Jonathan couldn't tell her the real reason he was there. He couldn't tell her that he was on the hunt for the little USB cipher drive. He wasn't about to blow his cover that quickly. But as he sat there staring at the woman in the early evening hours, he couldn't help but notice just how striking she was. Her high cheekbones and slender frame, combined with her luscious lips and pale blue eyes, gave Jonathan that feeling in his stomach that he felt when he was incredibly attracted to a woman. He tried to hide his clear interest in her from a sexual point of view.

"I never wanted to get involved with that project. They approached me to help them with some advanced algorithm computations for secure socket layers, or SSL, the standard data encryption method on the Internet."

"Who approached you?" Jonathan asked.

"Advanced Biogenics. It's a lab out of Arlington, Virginia. They're on the leading edge of some of the most revolutionary research in the field of genetics and mathematics. As a Harvard Fellow, I thought it would be a great addition to my resume, and I was excited by the possibility of publishing a paper based on my research."

"Well, what happened? Why was it such a bad idea, then?" Jonathan watched her cross her legs again. Her skinny jeans snapped fit to her elongated legs. Jonathan couldn't keep his eyes off of them. She met his stare ogling her figure multiple times. He couldn't help himself. Even though she looked closed off, her body language indicated she wasn't telling the truth. He became infatuated with her as he sat there directly across the table. The glass tabletop made it easy enough for Jonathan to soak in every ounce of her body, from the legs on up.

"My eyes are up here, you know," she replied back.

"I'm… I'm so sorry. I didn't mean to…"

"It's okay. I'm used to it by now. You can only imagine what I have to endure living here. I'm like a magnet for predators around here," she said. She nodded at the street filled with people walking by, most of whom were devouring her with their eyes just as Jonathan had been doing.

"I'm really sorry about that. I didn't know… I mean… I don't know what I want to say here. I'm not usually like this. Honestly."

"That's okay. I get it. You're a man. You can't help yourself." She uncrossed, then recrossed her legs, switching from the right to the left side as she leaned back into the chair.

Jonathan cracked a half-smile, but he didn't feel

comfortable with himself. He didn't feel right for looking at her the way he was, but he couldn't help himself. She was his ideal: Smart, and sexy. Then again, she was probably every man's ideal.

"Anyhow," she continued, disrupting his very sexual train of thought, "The research was some of the most exciting stuff that I had ever worked on, until the parameters changed. The goals of the project changed from something so simple and innocent, to something much more complex and calculated."

"What do you mean? Calculated, how?"

"Well, it started harmlessly enough. The SSL research was merely an extension of my advanced algorithm ciphers that that have been the subject of my obsessive post-doctoral work for the past five years. But, it got so much more involved when they reclassified the project, and quarantined me at the lab. I had no life back then and I wasn't allowed to leave. I was basically a slave to that lab."

"What happened with the research? How far did you get with it?"

"Well, pretty far. It was revolutionary, in fact. Within the first 6 months at the lab, I created an advanced algorithm cipher that could penetrate any 1024-bit RSA key security level. I thought we were working on prevention, of course, but my research made it possible for penetration into any system. I thought we were going to extend that research into advancing the RSA levels of security, but they wanted more from me."

"I did some research on the 1024-bit RSA key crack. I haven't been able to find any information that shows it's hackable. From current computing standards, it would take 7-months to brute-force attack and crack a 1024-bit RSA key." Jonathan looked at her with a puzzled expression. He knew there was a lot more to the whole story that he just wasn't grasping or that she wasn't telling him. So much of it was over his head, but he made it his duty to understand just what it all meant.

"That's what it used to be, until I developed my advanced algorithm coupling mechanism. What used to take 7 months could now be done in under 30 minutes. But there's more."

"More?"

"Yes," she replied, "they wanted me to continue my research to extend my algorithms into breaking a 2048-bit RSA key, something that could break into the highest possible levels of security on the Web for years to come. That's what they made me work on for a year in that lab."

"And? Did you actually do it? Did you figure it out?"

"Yes, but I wasn't allowed to leave the research facility until it was all completed. Don't get me wrong, they paid me very well for the project, but I have nothing to show for it. I wasn't allowed to publish any papers on the subject of my research and everything was kept very hush-hush."

Jonathan looked on as she spoke. He paid careful attention to the words that were coming out of her mouth. In fact, he also paid very careful attention to her mouth as well. She could have been a model for all he knew. That's how pretty she was, he thought in his mind. *Get a hold of yourself. Stop obsessing.*

"I have to tell you that it's all very intriguing to me," Jonathan replied, picking up the menu to look at what else the café offered.

"Well, I'm glad you're intrigued," she said with an air of sarcasm. "Is that why we're here? *Because I intrigue you?* Or is it the work that you're intrigued with?"

She had caught him off guard. He was never good around women, especially beautiful women. And, it had been so long since he had truly interacted with a beautiful woman like her. He had closed himself off for years after his wife passed. He didn't quite know what to say, but he just blurted out the first thing that came to his mind. "Both."

She smiled at that and almost laughed. Did she think he was funny or was she flirting with him? "I'm terrible at this. I'm usually not so clumsy with my words. Maybe I need a drink. Say, how come there's no alcohol on this menu?"

"You won't find alcohol on most of these menus. Remember, this is primarily a Muslim country. If you want alcohol, we would probably have to go to a hookah lounge or a proper restaurant nearby. It's just that these mainstream cafes won't carry it here, and if you ask them, you'll be insulting them."

So much was different in Turkey. Something that was so readily available in every corner store in the United States couldn't be purchased the same way. "What about bars and clubs? Does Istanbul have any of those?"

"Of course it does. It's just different when it comes to cafes here like this on a main boulevard like this one. A fancy restaurant here will have it and so will the hookah lounges, but not the cafes."

"Oh, makes sense, I suppose," he said.

"It's still readily available here. Just not exactly like it is in the states. Make sense?"

"Yeah. That makes sense. What do you say we head to a hookah lounge, or possibly a bar? I'm always much better when I have a few drinks." Of course, that was a lie. The last thing Jonathan needed to do was to have a drink. That was the last thing he ever needed to do.

"I can't tonight. How about tomorrow night? Saturday night."

"Okay, deal."

"How long are you here for?" she asked.

"Until I can finish the job."

"What's the job exactly, then?" she asked, looking at him with a new sense of suspect.

"I can't really say exactly." He was playing hard to get and it was annoying her just enough to be more curious.

"Well, clearly it has something to do with my research. I have a few guesses."

"Yes, of course it has to do something with your research," he said in response.

"Okay. Well, I have to get going. I'll see you tomorrow night," she said.

"See you then."

7

Somewhere along the French Riviera, off the coast of Monaco, Boris Medviek's superyacht cut through the waters at full throttle. The powerful, yet silent motors of the vessel raced through international waters, slicing through waves like a hot knife through butter. The sleek, audacious piece of machinery vaulted forward with the ease of a gliding bird as it catapulted its passengers and crew across the sea with careless intent. Boris walked out to the rear of the upper deck with a pair of binoculars and peered with a watchful eye out towards the shore. His constant paranoia had increased at a rampant pace since he had taken position of the USB cipher drive.

"What do you think of all this, Dmitry?" he asked.

They were standing in the twilight of the setting sun, and something just didn't feel right to Boris. The plan felt too good to be true. He had accomplished so much but still felt so far away. He knew that uneasy feeling meant something bad was on the horizon. Anytime he felt that uneasiness on the inside, something was bound to go wrong. He figured it was just a matter of time. He tried to think about the severity of the situation. He tried to balance it all in his mind. He had a vision of what he wanted, but there was so much involved. So many people to appease were standing in his way. It wasn't about the money any more. It hadn't been about the money for a long time. It was about the rush of the heist. He wanted to make a name for himself. He wanted his name to be remembered forever.

Dmitry looked out towards the coastal shores of Monaco. The yellow lights of the city at sunset reflected beautifully in the deep blue ocean waters of the Costa Azzura. "I think you and I have been talking about this day for a long time now," said Dmitry. "This is going to change everything, you know? The supply of money will be endless. Just imagine what we can do with it," he said.

Boris held onto the chromed hand railing at the aft of

the ship as he watched the ocean disappearing behind them, leaving a large ripple in its wake. He watched the dancing colors in the sky as the sun dipped behind the ocean in the distance. As they traveled west, he realized just how perfect it all was. He wanted to bottle up that moment in time and savor it forever.

As he stood there watching the sun and talking to his comrade, Boris rolled up the sleeves to his white linen dress shirt. "Yes, brother, we can do very much with it," he replied. "But think of the power this will give us. People will bow down to us. No one can stop us. Not even armies. Nothing. Do you realize that?"

The younger brother, Dmitry, had envied Boris for a long time. He had always looked up to his older and smarter brother, and he realized just how much he had accomplished in such a short period of time. But, there was still so much that had to be done. He reveled in the power the cipher drive brought. Without it, he would be crippled, and he would do anything in his power to ensure no one else got their hands on it. Anything.

"What about the doctor? She knows too much," Dmitry said. His sullen look struck a nerve with Boris. He knew that Dmitry was right. She was the only one who knew how the algorithms worked. She was the one who had devised them and the one that could replicate them again if she chose to. They needed to eliminate all of the variables in the equation. They couldn't allow any stone to go unturned.

"We don't have to worry about the doctor," She's not our problem. She doesn't know about us, and she couldn't replicate the black box without all the data from the lab. And, now that we all the data, the backups, and the hardware, no one can stand in our way." Boris clearly wasn't feeling the same way his brother was. He didn't think that the doctor could interfere with their plans.

"But, she's a threat brother, I assure you. Weren't you always the one to tell me that we should never underestimate people? We can't underestimate the doctor. We have to make sure that we tie up all the loose ends. We can't have extra baggage lying around out there. Even if she couldn't recreate the cipher drive without another year of work, it's her research that is the foundation for it. I think she's a threat brother."

"What do you suggest we do?" asked Boris.

They both stared out over the railing of the ship as they stood side by side, looking off into the distance. They soaked in the beauty of the region as the sun slowly set along the horizon. "I think we should send Viktor to take care of our little problem. We can tell him to keep it clean and make it quick."

Boris looked at his comrade. He wasn't quite sure that it was the right decision to do, but he didn't want to appear weak. "Where is the doctor?" he asked.

"Istanbul. They tell me she's in Istanbul."

"Da. Okay. Make the call."

"Okay, done," said Dmitry.

Dmitry walked off, leaving Boris there alone in the encroaching dark blue hues of the evening sky. The wind rushed through his hair as the vessel continued cutting through the waters, its engine rumbling beneath him. He listened to the sounds of the waves being sliced by the bow of the ship and he closed his eyes.

*****

On a passenger ferry steaming across the Sea of Marmara just south of Istanbul, Turkey, Jonathan Grace checked his watch. It was 5:52pm. He stood in the center of the boat and stretched his head out to check the boat's distance from the shore. Two hours and eight minutes before he met with Dr. Cobalt again. He watched as a thick flock of seagulls tracked the ferry gliding its way across the shimmering ancient body of water. The thick black chain that separated the mid-section of the ferry from the water held back the troves of passengers waiting to disembark at their destinations.

After a day of exploring and seeing the sights of Istanbul, he was relieved to be making more progress with Dr. Cobalt. He was going to get the nerve to ask her about the cipher drive. She had to know something about its whereabouts. He tightly gripped the strap of his nylon backpack that was slung over his shoulder and pulled it closer to his chest. As the sun kissed the top of a mosque far off in the distance, he prepared himself. He was ready. He knew what he was going to say and how he was going to say it. All day and night, he couldn't get that doctor out of his head. He couldn't get her long slender legs and her striking features out of his mind. Her beauty haunted him and gave him a feeling he hadn't felt in years.

He slipped his hand into his pocket and felt the silver USB stick Don Cicerone had given him as a reminder of what he had to do. He needed to remember why he was there in the first place. He couldn't get caught up with this woman just because he thought she was beautiful. But, as he held the silver USB stick between his thumb and his index finger, he couldn't help but think of her more. Why was he so drawn to her? What was it about her that was so intriguing? Surely, he wanted to know everything about her. But why?

He had to think more clearly. He had to pull himself together. And as the boat neared the dock at his destination, he looked out over the side again to take in the sights. The people pushed in towards the exit as the boat docked, and Jonathan disembarked to a sea of taxis waiting on the avenue alongside the docks. He hopped into a taxi and gave instructions to the cabbie that Dr. Cobalt had provided. She was at Istanbul University doing a lecture on Applied Mathematics, and he had agreed to meet up with her and drive to an area bar or lounge where they could continue their conversation over drinks.

As they drove along the docks and towards the Galata Bridge, the distinct smell of the salty sea rushed through the open car windows. The breeze felt good on Jonathan's face, and he smiled. It had been a long time since he had felt a sense of peace. Maybe getting out of New York was the best thing he could have done for himself. He closed his eyes and tried to think back to his dingy Brooklyn apartment. He tried to picture that place again and his mental state there. He wasn't happy there. He hadn't been happy for a long time. This was what he needed. He finally got the chance to travel and work at the same time. Life couldn't get any better, he thought. *It doesn't get any better than this.* They crossed the short Galata Bridge to the other side of the narrow strait. Based on his maps, the university was a 15-minute drive from where they were, so he whipped out his phone to check for messages. He had forwarded all of this phone calls from his number back home to the international number he had secured when he arrived. He dialed into the voicemail system that was setup on the new number. He had a message from Don Cicerone.

Kid. We gotta talk. Call me.

In the excitement of arriving in Turkey, he had forgotten to check in with Don Cicerone. He quickly dialed the number back.

"Hello?" said Vinnie on the other end.

"Hey, it's Jonathan Grace."

"Oh, hey. Hold a moment," he said, and passed the phone to Don Cicerone.

"Kid?"

"Yeah, I'm here," said Jonathan.

"What's the status? What's the scoop?"

"I located the doctor. In fact, I'm en route to meet with her right now."

"Don't screw this up kid. Word on the street is that the doc might be in hot water. Be careful."

"What do you mean?" If the Italians were telling him to be careful, then something must be wrong, he thought.

"Look, kid, just be careful. And, check in with me from time to time. I need to know what's going on. Also, don't you dare come back here without that cipher drive. I don't care what it takes."

"What do you mean?"

"You know what I mean kid. Look, come back with the cipher drive or it's your neck."

"Are you threatening me?"

He had already hung up the phone when Jonathan lobbed that last question. It was almost rhetorical. He knew he was being threatened. He wasn't sure why he had even asked that question. As he looked out the window again, almost in another world, the beauty of the city slipped through his hands and worry creeped in. When they finally pulled up to the University a few minutes later, he dialed Dr. Cobalt on the phone. She didn't answer, but she sent him a text asking him to come inside because she was wrapping up a lecture for a class that had started late.

Jonathan paid the cab and walked inside the university. He made his way through the hallways, following the directions on the text, and found the lecture room where Dr. Cobalt was teaching. He silently walked in and took a seat in the back. The students were so enthralled with the lecture that they barely noticed him slip through the door.

He sat there carefully watching her as she spoke. He couldn't understand the language, but he looked on with a silent determination. He was captivated by her liveliness. She was so energetic and enthusiastic.

When she finished up and the students left, he walked down to the front of the classroom from up the stairs in the back. "Hey," he said.

"Hi. I'm really sorry the class went over. I ended up getting in pretty late."

"It's okay. It was fascinating to watch you teach. I mean, I didn't quite understand a thing that you said, but I was still fascinated by it." Jonathan looked at all the formulas on the chalkboard that she was busy scribbling on during the lecture. "Hey, what is all of this stuff?"

"Just some advanced mathematics. Algorithms, some calculus, you know, boring stuff," she said. She laughed silently to herself, then touched her hand to her neck. He made her nervous.

Jonathan smiled back. "Looks like pretty advanced stuff. I'm sure most of this would just go right over my head."

"It's really not that complex when you get into it. I can imagine looking from the outside in, but it's not really that bad," she said. She had her hair in one of those long ponytails that made her look really casual. But, even in her attempt to look casual, she was still striking. Jonathan just stared at her. He couldn't help himself.

"What? What is it?" she asked.

"Oh… sorry… nothing. Do you want to go get that drink now?"

"Yeah. Sure, that sounds pretty good," she said.

As they walked out of the university together, she wrapped her elbow inside his, as if she wanted him to guide her out. Jonathan looked at her for a moment and butterflies filled his stomach. He smiled at her. They piled into her car and headed down the road. Within moments, they had arrived at the restaurant on the water.

"This is my favorite place to eat. I hope you like fish," she said.

"Yes, absolutely. I love fish."

"Then you're going to love this place," she cooed. "The fish here is fresh and it's caught the same day it's served. It's absolutely incredible."

They were seated on an outdoor raised terrace overlooking the water, which was separated from the restaurant by a two-way road. "Wow, it's incredible here," Jonathan said. "The view."

"I know. I love it here. Isn't Turkey beautiful?" she asked.

"Yes. In fact, ever since I arrived, I've felt so much more alive. It was as if I was dead back home. Does that make sense?"

"How so?" she asked.

"I don't know. I guess I've just felt dead inside lately. The past couple of years have been rough on me."

"Oh. I'm sorry. Do you want to talk about it?"

Actually, Jonathan didn't want to talk about that. He just wanted to talk about her. He wanted to know everything about her he could possibly find out. He was so intrigued by her. Her beauty. Her intellect. Everything about her attracted him; everything about her sung to his heart. "Two years ago, I lost my wife to cancer."

"Oh. Oh my. I'm so… I'm… I'm really sorry. That's just terrible. How long were you… how long were the two of you?"

"It was hard," he replied softly. "It was really hard. In fact, it was the hardest thing I ever had to go through my entire life. I guess you just don't imagine how something like that could ever happen to you until it does. It was as if she went from being completely fine to crippled and unable to care for herself within a three-month period. I lost her so fast. It was almost as if, as soon as she found out about it, she all but gave up. It was as if she just threw in the towel and quit when the doctor gave us the bad news. It was hard. You should have seen her. You should have seen the look on her face when the doctor told us. It was as if she had seen a ghost; her own ghost."

Jennifer put her hand to her mouth. The news was heartbreaking. She had never lost anyone close to her. She wasn't sure what to say. She wasn't sure how she was supposed to respond. She looked into his big brown eyes and admired his boyish good looks. "I'm so sorry… that sounds… awful," she added.

"It was awful. You couldn't even imagine how bad something like that could be until it happens to you. And seeing that cancer take hold and suck the energy out of someone… you don't realize the power of it until you see it. It was awful. I can't tell you just how awful it was."

She reached over and placed her hand on top of his. She looked into his eyes. He had such big brown puppy-dog eyes. And, she felt sorry for him. She utterly and truly felt sorrow deep down inside for him. All she could do was look at him. She just continued to look at him with sorrow in her eyes for him. "That makes me feel sick to my stomach."

"I'm sorry I'm bringing up all of this sad stuff. We barely know each other and here I am pouring my heart out to you. I'm so silly."

"No. Please don't say that," she said. She threw him an exaggerated frown and squeezed his hand.

"But really...what I really want to know more about is you. Tell me about you. Ever since I met you, I've just wanted to know more about you. I know that sounds strange," he said.

She smiled at him and then turned her head towards the ocean. She was distracted by something. It was as if something was bothering her; something was eating away at her. Jonathan could see it in her eyes. There was this emptiness and he related to that. He didn't know exactly what it was. He didn't know exactly how to put his finger on it. Ever since he met her in person, he could sense it.

"Merhaba, hoşgeldiniz," said a server who appeared before them. Jonathan smiled politely.

"Merhaba," he said back.

"Ne Içiyorsunuz?" asked the server.

Jonathan looked a little dumbfounded. The words were a little beyond his comprehension of the Turkish language.

"What do you want to drink?" Jennifer asked with a wink.

"Oh, maybe a bottle of red wine? Do you like wine?" he asked her.

"Yes," she said. She turned her attention to the waiter and did some ordering in Turkish. "I'll order us some food too," she told him. "They usually bring out small plates here. Almost like tapas style. You'll love it."

"Great," he said.

The wine and appetizers landed in front of them. The assortment of cheeses in small dishes, along with a variety of meats and small fried appetizers, looked delicious to him. Then came the fish. He ogled the plate in front of him like a man who had just suffered through the perils of a long and arduous famine.

"Wow," Jonathan said.

"I just ordered some small starter plates, then a few main course plates. Everything is delicious," she added, dishing out some of the food onto her own plate.

"It looks that way." Jonathan virtually shoveled food into his mouth. He certainly looked famished. He tried to eat slowly but he never could. He always had a hard time savoring things like food. He seemed to rush through life at such a breakneck pace. He knew he needed to slow down. He knew that. But he never seemed to be able to do it. "This food… it's… it's incredible. I'm sorry I'm eating like a pig."

"No, it's quite alright," she said. "Please don't apologize.

I'm glad that you're enjoying it."

"Yes, definitely. Thank you for bringing me here. I guess there's nothing like having a local take you to their favorite restaurant in town is there?"

"No, there probably isn't," she said, smiling at him as she placed another morsel of food into her mouth.

"So, did you grow up here? What's you're connection to Turkey?"

"Well, don't you know?" she asked. "I mean you tracked me down and all. I figured you would have known everything about me," she added.

"Well… no… I mean… I… I don't," he said, stumbling for words.

"Yes. To answer your question, I am from here," she said. "I moved to the states to attend university and get my doctorate degree. I've lived there for 15 years and only recently took a small sabbatical back home here, to Istanbul. My mom is starting to get to that age where I really need to spend more time with her. I've always wanted her to come to the states, but it's too late for that now. Her English isn't very good. All my immediate family is here."

"How about your husband?" Jonathan asked. He looked for a ring but couldn't find one so he knew she wasn't married, but he was curious about her past.

"I'm not currently married except to my work. It's hard to find the time to balance a relationship with my work schedule. It's always so taxing to be able to keep a social life, let alone have a husband in my line of work." She seemed distant as she said the words, as if there was something she wasn't telling him. He didn't feel like she was lying to him, but just that she was maybe leaving some things out.

"I don't understand. How could someone as beautiful as you have never been married before? That's hard to believe."

"Well, I didn't say that I was never married, just that I'm not married right now. I was married… yes… I was and I would rather not talk about it," she said as she scooped another morsel of food into her mouth.

"Oh, I'm sorry. I didn't mean to upset you… I mean… I understand that you don't want to talk about it," he said.

"No, that's okay. Don't apologize. I didn't mean to come across rude. I guess there's just certain things that… I would rather not think about right now," she said.

"I understand. I guess I still can't believe that you're not in a relationship or something. I'm sorry I'm probably just stumbling on my own words. I feel silly." Jonathan eyed a piece of fish on his plate, and placed it in his mouth. It melted like butter and he had to close his eyes to finish savoring it.

"No. It's okay. Believe it or not, balancing a relationship with my kind of work is hard. People don't seem to be able to understand the passion that I have for my work. I've been called everything from selfish, self-entitled, mean, and everything in-between. It's really not worth it for me. Relationships really haven't been worth my while. I guess if I had met 'Mr. Right," so-to-speak, maybe…maybe things would have been different."

Jonathan had a hard time believing that the stunning beauty sitting before him wasn't married or in a relationship. He realized there was probably a lot there that he just wasn't seeing because he was too blinded by her beauty. He knew that it could get him into hot water, but he continued to stare at her like a teenager with a crush. She could tell he was into her. She could tell how much he was attracted to her, but she was used to that. She was used to the unwanted advances of men throughout all of her life.

"Tell me more about your work. I'm fascinated by it. Seeing you there, teaching, at the university, was inspiring. I've never met someone like you before. I guess that's what it is," he said. He raised his glass to meet hers and stared straight into her pale blue eyes. "Cheers," he added.

"Cheers," she said. "About my work? I guess you already know a lot about it. I'm very much into applied mathematics and advanced algorithms. I spent a couple of years in the lab in Virginia working day and night, and I guess I got burnt out, which is why I came back here."

"What exactly were you doing there?"

"I was working on a project, which I told you about, but it got out of hand. Everything got out of hand. The pressure was unbearable but the pay was terrific. I was always married to my job, but this was extreme even for my own standards. I was working day and night, and would literally only go home to sleep. I woke up the next day and did it all over again. It was a never-ending cycle. I felt trapped. I'm so happy that's over with for now. Right now, all I want to do is just relax, spend time with family, and catch my breath."

It was the exact opposite of how Jonathan had been living his life. He almost felt guilty for living in such utter disregard for others, and for himself. He hadn't worked hard at all; he was just on a downward spiral that seemed to have no end in sight.

"How about you?" she asked.

"Me?"

"Yeah, what's you're deal? Why are you really here? I

know you didn't come all the way over here just to track me down just so that you could get to know me better."

"Well… I'm looking for something."

"Oh," she said, but she didn't look surprised.

"I'm looking for something you helped to create," he said. He took a big swig of his wine and poured himself another glass.

"And what's that?"

"The cipher drive. I'm looking for the cipher drive. Jen, you're in danger and I need to find the cipher drive."

"Well… I don't have it."

"Who does?"

"I don't know. It was taken from the lab in Virginia. All I know is that they told me it was stolen from there after my work had been completed; after I had already left the country. I'm not about to go back now. It's their problem. I did my job. I did the work that they forced me to do."

"Forced? Stolen? By whom?" Jonathan wondered if it was the Italians who stole it. But, if they had stolen it, then someone must have stolen it from them. He hated being in the dark about the information. He hated not knowing what really was going on. He realized he should have prepared better for the meeting. He should have asked more questions and done more research. He started feeling stupid and sorry for himself.

"I don't know who stole it. I have no idea," she said. "All I know is that whoever has the cipher drive, if they know just how to use it, it could be catastrophic."

"What do you mean?"

"Think about it, Jon – that cipher drive has an advanced-algorithm deciphering system that can crack the most advanced RSA secure server technology through brute force in under 30 minutes. Do you know what that means? Could you imagine what someone could do with that technology?"

"Isn't that what hackers can already do today?"

"No. It doesn't work that way. Hackers usually use sophisticated measures of phishing to gain employee access credentials to servers. Then, they get in and do their best to do the most amount of damage as quickly as possible, but once it's discovered, the game is usually over. This is different. This is a method of hacking using brute force attacks on secure servers. It doesn't matter if the hacker has credentials. As long as they have an IP address for the machine, they can force their way inside. Normally, this is not that easy, especially when you're dealing with the ultra-secure servers that are load-balanced to withstand brute-force attacks. This goes after the secure layer, and it's very effective. With that cipher drive, and the right person operating it, you can hack anything. Any database in the world can be broken into. Think about it – financial intuitions, government institutions, the NSA, the CIA, the FBI, any Fortune 500 company, anything Jon."

Jonathan sat back in his chair as she spoke to him. He tried to understand the gravity of what she was saying. No wonder the Italians wanted to pay him a million dollars for that thing. They could use it to swipe billions upon billions of dollars if they knew what they were doing. And he was sure that was their intention. But knowing that now, Jonathan was at a loss for what to do. Should he help the mob get the cipher drive back or not?

"That's crazy. So you helped to build a device to hack any computer system in the world?"

"Well, I didn't know what the intent was at first. The initial specs of the project, like I had told you before, were to find the vulnerabilities in the RSA key at the 1024-bit level. But, when I did that and we moved onto the 2048-bit level, I guess I had an assumption that's what the intent was."

"And you didn't say something? You didn't do anything to stop it? Why, if you knew, did you continue to help them?" Jonathan was searching her eyes for an answer to the question. Why would she have gone along with a project that she knew was bad? What was her motivation in it all? It wasn't adding up.

"It's a legitimate lab and it was part of my research…part of my passion," she said, stumbling for words. "I didn't realize it was going to fall into the wrong hands. Plus, they paid me really well for the job. I mean, it would have taken me 20 years of work to make the same amount of money I made in that 2-year span," she said.

Jonathan looked at her. Something wasn't making sense. She wasn't telling him everything. He felt like she was leaving something out, but he just didn't know exactly what it was. He was an expert at reading body language, and he analyzed all the signals. He looked at her gestures and her expressions, and he knew that she wasn't being completely honest with him. He knew that she wasn't telling the complete truth. He took another big gulp of his wine as he tried to digest the gravity of the situation. He looked out towards the water to watch the beautiful colors dancing in the sky.

"That sunset… look at the colors," he said, trying to change the subject and not seem so combative.

"I know. It's beautiful, isn't it?"

"I never realized this country could be so beautiful."

"Yes. Yes, well, it is. This is home. This is my home." She spoke silently as she finished off her glass of wine and looked out toward the water. The remaining entrees arrived and the waiter topped off their wine glasses. After they were finished eating, they walked toward her car.

"That was delicious," he said. He stared at her pale blue eyes. She was almost his height with her high heels on. She was only an inch or so shorter, and he couldn't help but take her all in. He looked at her with this lost longing that he hadn't felt in a long time. He had masked his pain and agony for years, but in that very moment, he almost felt like he was meant to be there. It was as if he had been destined to go to that place. At least that's what he thought to himself.

"I know. I love it here. So, where are you staying? I can drop you off," she said.

"I'm staying in Besiktas. Is that how you pronounce it?"

She smiled. "No, well, not exactly. It sounds different than it looks. It's pronounced 'Beshiktash'. The line under the letter 's' is pronounced with a 'sh' sound. So Beşiktaş is pronounced Beshiktash."

"Oh, okay," he said.

As they were about to hop into her two-door ten-year old blue BMW, a black SUV with tinted windows roared around the corner, coming at them head on. Jennifer's car was parked next to a stone wall that supported the raised terrace of the restaurant that they just finished having dinner at. The SUV was traveling fast, its engine revving as it gunned the throttle towards them. In a split second move, Jonathan grabbed Jennifer and pulled her aside just in time as the SUV knocked out the side-view mirror of the car and rammed into the driver door of the car behind them before speeding off.

"What the hell!?" she yelled. They were both breathing hard as they looked back at the SUV as it slammed on its brakes and spun back around. This time it was coming at them even faster.

"Hurry up, give me the keys!" Jonathan yelled at her. A few people had gathered atop the terrace and looked down at the SUV as it gunned its engine and sped back towards them. Jonathan was in a panic. "Shit! Come on."

This time as the SUV approached, it lowered its passenger window. Jonathan could see the barrel of a silencer as an olive-skinned man with silver aviator lenses pointed it towards them and fired. Jonathan pulled her down behind the car just in time as the gunshots grazed them and the slugs lodged into the wall behind them.

"Shit!" Jennifer yelled. The people on the terrace above

screamed, as the SUV gunned its engine and passed them again. "Here… here are the keys!" she yelled and threw them at him. He ran to the driver's side door, breathing heavy. He was in a panic. What the hell was going on? Someone was trying to kill them. Someone was after them. They knew he was there. They knew where she was.

He threw the car into reverse and slammed hard into the car behind them. The sound of crunching steel erupted as the two cars banged into one another. Then, he threw the car forward and lurched out of the very tight parking spot against the stone wall, pushing the car in front of them just enough to escape into the right of way. Jonathan gunned the engine of the compact BMW as the SUV headed straight towards them in the narrow strip that was encased by parked cars on both sides. They were playing chicken on that small side road, and Jonathan could hear the thumping beat of his heart in the back of his throat. He could feel the dampness seep into his hands as he gripped the steering wheel at 10 and 2 o'clock. He pushed the throttle down harder and the car lunged forward towards the SUV.

As the two vehicles approached one another, the man thrust a gun from the driver's side window and fired towards them. Jonathan pushed her head down and ducked below the steering wheel as the gunshots rattled through the windshield. Five shots made their way into the car as it neared them. Jonathan careened into the parked cars on the right side of the street, against the stone wall, and both vehicles crunched into one another as they sped by in opposite directions.

"Oh my God! Shit! Are you okay? Talk to me. Are you okay?" he asked. He was in a panic and breathing harder than ever. His knuckles had turned white and his heart dropped into his stomach as he gripped the steering wheel with dear life.

She was bleeding from her shoulder. He could see the blood coming out of her, and he started cursing. "I've been shot," she said. She spoke ominously, as she looked at her shoulder to see the blood. She was in a state of shock.

"We have to stop the bleeding he yelled." He was trying to pay attention to her as he navigated the car through the side road. When he came upon the exit to the major thoroughfare that ran along the ocean, he slammed on the brakes, spun the car left, then right into the lane, barely missing another vehicle. He could see the SUV gaining on them from behind. It had to stop at the entrance to the thoroughfare because of the cars that blocked its way. He could hear the driver of the SUV honking its horn in a fit of rage.

Jonathan didn't hesitate. He didn't want to waste any time. He revved the engine faster as he took off his shirt and tied a tight knot around Jennifer's wound.

"We have to get you to a hospital… we have to…"

"No," she said. "No hospitals. They will know to look there. We can't… we can't go there. We have to go somewhere else. I have a friend… he's a doctor. He lives about an hour from here. We have to go there…"

Jonathan looked at her. She could tell she was fading fast. The color was leaving her face, and she was turning as white as a ghost. He looked in the rearview mirror and could the see the SUV accelerating as it came around the bend in an effort to catch up with them. He swerved in and out of the lanes, pushing past cars that honked at him violently as he raced his way through the light congestion of the oceanside road.

"Which way? Which way do I go? Are you still with me?" Jonathan shook her by the leg. He tried to get her to stay with him. She couldn't lose consciousness. If she did, he wouldn't know where to go. He wouldn't know how to get there.

Jennifer's eyes were slightly opened, but they were closing rapidly. Each time she had an elongated blink, her eyelids would stay shut for a second or two before she opened them back up again. She looked out at the road with her eyes half opened and pointed out the direction. "It's… it's up that way," she said. She pointed to an exit that headed inland from the ocean. She pointed to the right in a general direction. "It's in that direction," she said again.

Jonathan could see that she was fading fast. He stepped on the gas, but he didn't know where he was going. He threw the car into third gear from fourth and redlined the engine as he gunned past another two cars, swerving left, then right. He could see the SUV close on his tail. Just as soon as he passed the car to the right, and as the SUV tried to follow suit, Jonathan quickly swerved again just narrowly making the next exit. The SUV was stuck behind a car and missed the exit. Jonathan could see him slamming on his brakes as he took the ramp, curving up and off to the right, inland, away from the beach and the crazed murderer.

"Which way from here? Are you still with me? God, please be okay. Just hold on for me. Hold on until we get there," he said. He was still in a panic. He kept one hand on the wheel, the other on her shoulder, squeezing the shirt tight around her wound to suppress the bleeding. He had to switch back and forth just to change the gears as the perspiration ran down the side of his face. Jonathan raced the car up a hill and screeched around another corner as she pointed in the general direction. He couldn't slow down. He wouldn't slow down. He had never been shot at before.

His mind was racing a million-miles-a-minute. He could feel the thumping of his heart in the back of his throat. He swallowed down hard as he tried to keep his nerve. He was trying to hold back the tears as he looked at her lying there helpless. They drove on like that for twenty more minutes before he felt like they were in the clear. He didn't spot the SUV again, but that didn't mean that it wouldn't reappear. He knew that if someone wanted to find her badly enough, they would, and he couldn't let that happen. He couldn't let anything happen to her. Something inside of him wanted to protect her. He was sent there to extract information from her, but all he wanted to do was keep her safe at that moment in time.

"Down this road," she said. "Turn down this road." Barely able to speak, she pointed to a street that ran up a steep hill to the right, which was lined by new apartment buildings. The street was narrow, and the cobblestones were more pronounced as they got further up the hill. They rounded the corner at the top and sped down another two streets before coming upon the block where her doctor friend was located. "I hope he's home. Park there, in that underground." She was in excruciating pain. The bleeding had all but stopped but Jonathan could tell that she was fiercely fighting back tears. He could see the terror in her eyes.

"Who the hell was that?" he asked her.

"I don't know. I have no idea. But I would be dead if it wasn't for you. I panicked and froze. You helped me." Jennifer turned her head to look at him while he was driving, and it was the first time she felt a twinge of something for a complete stranger that had protected her. She felt like he was her guardian angel at that moment. "You saved me," she said. "You saved me… I can't begin to thank you enough." She had tears in her eyes. Jonathan could see that she was trying her best to keep it together.

"We're not out of the woods yet," he said. "We need to hide this car."

"Here, just park in the underground here. I have the code. Punch in 2-3-8-5 on the keypad," she said.

He pulled up to a keypad, punched the keys, and it opened up a large garage dedicated to the building. The car would be much safer underground than it was out on the city streets. But the bullet holes in the windshield needed to be fixed or they needed to ditch the car. He didn't know what he was going to do, but his first priority was to get her patched up. Right then, that's all he could think about. He would worry about the rest later.

8

"We've had some complications," said the voice on the other end of the line. Dmitry listened carefully to the man he entrusted to kill the doctor. It was exactly what he didn't want to hear. It was exactly what he didn't want to report back to his brother either.

"Complications?" asked Dmitry. He couldn't believe that the job hadn't been done. He was furious. Boris looked at his brother as he spoke on the phone, and he could see him turning red with anger. He knew his brother all too well. He knew just how hot-tempered he was.

"Yes. The girl. She wasn't alone. She's with someone," said Viktor.

"What do you mean she's not alone? This was a simple job. You were supposed to take out the girl. That was all – plain and simple. What happened?"

"Someone interrupted the plans. Someone helped her, and they got away. They lost me in the city streets. I'm sorry. It won't happen again. I'll fix this," Viktor said, barking back into the phone. His mind was spinning and he was furious. He didn't need the bad reputation this would give him.

"What the hell do you mean, they lost you? What the hell is that supposed to mean?!" Dmitry was yelling into the phone now. His face went from red to purple, and the veins in the side of his neck and forehead were pulsating with anger.

"Brother, calm down," said Boris. Boris placed a hand on his shoulder to subdue his hot-tempered brother. "Relax."

"I can't relax brother," he said. He yelled back into the phone then hung up. "I'm sorry, I screwed this up," Dmitry said as Boris listened with mild temperament. "I take full responsibility. My guy messed up. I'm sorry. I don't know what to say."

"It's okay. Nothing is screwed up. We'll get the doctor," Boris said. He was calm, cool, and collected, exactly opposite Dmitry's disposition. The two balanced each other out in that way.

"You don't understand. She has help. She's with someone. Someone is helping her. This is more important now than ever. We have to get her. We have to find her. This is a loose end we can't afford to have, brother." Dmitry was sweating in the cool night. Boris could see the perspiration on his forehead as they sat in the large living area of the superyacht as it continued cutting through international waters.

"What do you want to do, brother?" asked Boris.

"We need to find her. We need to find her now. You need to do your magic. You need to hack into the Turkish healthcare systems and find out where she is and if she checked into a hospital. I need all the information that I can get on her. I want to know where she spends her time and who she spends it with. We'll find her like that. We'll force her to surface, even if Viktor can't. Tell me you'll do this, brother."

"Of course. That's the easy part. I can get the information, but not over the satellite linkup. We should to get to land. Let's head back inland and dock. We'll change course towards Istanbul. We can dock in port there. We're not far from there."

"Okay, brother. I agree. Let's do that."

*****

"What floor?" Jonathan supported Jennifer by her right shoulder – the good shoulder – and helped her towards the elevator.

"Fifteen. Apartment 1531."

They hobbled into the elevator together. Jonathan propped her up against the side railing and hit the button. The elevator lurched up, making an incessant whining noise the whole way to the top floor. "Who is this guy, anyway? How do you know him?"

"He's a friend of the family. He's a medical doctor. We've known each other since we were kids. He can help and it won't get logged into any hospital database."

"Do you trust him?"

"Yes, with my life," she said.

"Okay, okay."

Jonathan led her toward the apartment, and they knocked on the door with three quick thuds. A man came to the door and said something in Turkish, and Jennifer replied. He quickly opened the door and she almost collapsed into his arms."

"Ne oldu ya?" he asked in Turkish. Jonathan assumed it meant what was happening or what had happened. They started speaking in Turkish rapidly, and Jonathan was lost in translation. He couldn't understand what was being said and eventually stopped trying to listen to the conversation. He led them to the bedroom where they laid her down and pulled off her shirt.

"This is my friend Mehmet," Jennifer said.

"Nice to meet you," he said in English. "What happened?" he asked.

"Thank god you speak English. We were shot at. Is she going to be okay?" Jonathan asked.

He took off her shirt and Jonathan couldn't help but stare. He looked into her pale blue eyes and had it not been for all the blood, he would have most likely been floored by the fact that he was seeing her in a black lace bra. He was surprised that she wore such a racy bra that day. Jonathan quickly pulled his mind out of the gutter, resisting its natural urge to go there.

"Don't judge me," she said, trying her best to crack a smile.

"I'm not judging. I am admiring." Jonathan tried to make light of the situation, but considering the circumstances, he was struggling with what he was supposed to say at a moment like that.

"The bullet is lodged in there. I have to get it out first," Mehmet said. "Here, prop her head up with this. I'm going to get some fresh towels and my medical kit."

The doctor disappeared for a few moments and Jonathan kneeled down beside the bed in the large room. "Thank God he was home," he said to her. "You're going to be okay."

"I know. Thankfully he was here. Jonathan, I'm frightened. What am I going to do? Where am I going to go?"

"Don't worry about that right now. Don't focus on that. Just focus on healing, and we'll figure it out. I'm not going to let anything bad happen to you. I promise."

"Thank you," she said.

He reached out and held her hand, and looked into her pale blue eyes. Those eyes. He was mesmerized by those eyes. But, as he was lost in her eyes, Mehmet reappeared with fresh towels and a bowl of hot water, along with his supplies.

"Okay, this is going to hurt," he said.

"Should I stay?" Jonathan asked.

"Yes, yes. Stay. I am going to need your help." The doctor had a grave look of concern on his face as he pulled out a large needle. "This is local anesthetic. It will numb the pain a little bit. He positioned the needle over the vein in the crevice of her arm by her bicep, and quickly stuck it in. Jonathan watched as the liquid drained from the needle and into her arm. He could see a calm wash over her face.

"Okay, you have to help me hold these instruments, and give them to me as I ask for them. He slipped on some rubber gloves and went to work trying to dislodge the bullet from Jennifer's shoulder. He had a very serious look of concern during the entire procedure. Jonathan could feel the anxiety perspiring off the doctor has he worked diligently to dislodge the bullet. Jonathan handed him his instruments as he cut into her shoulder and pulled the bullet out with a pair of medical pliers. Jonathan cringed at the sight and had to look away.

"There. I got it," the doctor said.

"Is she going to be okay?"

"Let's hope so. She's lost a lot of blood. I have to stitch her up. Hand me the needle from there and the suture string please. It's a black string in a small roll."

"Here you go," Jonathan said.

The doctor worked to stitch her up. Jennifer was nearly passed out the entire time. She kept trying to open her eyes, and Jonathan kept a cool rag on her forehead, telling her it was going to be okay. But, he didn't know for sure if it was going to be okay. He didn't know what to think anymore. He was scared and it was obvious. He tried his best to hide his fears. He tried his best to keep his cool.

"There. That's it. That's the last one," Mehmet said. "Now, she needs to rest. Here, take these." He placed two pills in her mouth and told her to swallow. "It's for the pain. She needs to rest."

The doctor led Jonathan out of the bedroom, and they closed the door to allow her some time to sleep it off. The pain medication was going to hit hard. Jennifer's body was most likely going to shut down and she could sleep it off. He led Jonathan into the living area where he got a first glimpse out onto the city.

"Wow, we're really high up here. You can see the entire city from this point," Jonathan said. "I didn't even notice it when we first came in."

"Yes, we're at the top of a very steep hill at the highest elevation in the city. You can see the Bosporus from here. You see the Bosporus Bridge over there?" Mehmet pointed to the beautiful bridge that was cast over the Bosporus Strait. It looked majestic from there. Everything looked majestic. Mosques dotted the horizon. They were everywhere.

"Wow, this is beautiful," Jonathan said.

"I'm glad you like it."

"Have you lived here long?"

"Three years now."

"How do you and Jennifer know each other?"

"We went to secondary school together here in Istanbul. We've known each other for about 20 years now." They walked over and sat in two armchairs in front of the floor-to-ceiling windows. "Would you like some kave?"

"I'm sorry? Kave?"

"Yes, that's Turkish for coffee," Mehmet said.

"Sure, I would love some."

"It's strong coffee, however. It's similar to say a double espresso in the states."

"Sure, yes. I love espresso. I haven't had a chance to try the coffee here yet."

"I'm sure you'll like it," Mehmet said.

Mehmet disappeared for a few minutes while Jonathan sat there taking in the stunning landscape. He hadn't seen the city from that point of view and it was picturesque from up there. He couldn't remember another city as beautiful as that. The twinkling lights of the Bosporus Bridge were reflected in the water as the sun disappeared in the sky. The Bosporus Bridge changed colors every few moments from red, to orange, to blue. Mehmet reappeared with the coffee and served it in two small glasses that looked like miniature mugs.

"You know that in Turkish tradition, women will usually tell your horoscope with the grains of the coffee. When you're finished, you would flip it over and wait a few moments. As the coffee-sludge runs down the sides of the cup, it leaves pictures there that are then interpreted. These women use those pictures to tell a person's future or horoscope using the coffee cup."

"That's interesting," Jonathan said.

"Yes, and some women are very good at it." The doctor smiled as they sipped their coffee. "Do you like it? I know it's late for coffee, but in Turkey, we drink coffee at all hours."

"Yes, I like it. But, as you said it's very strong."

"Yes, one or two of these and you'll be bouncing off the walls." They both laughed. "So, tell me again, what's going on here? I'm very worried for my friend. You know, this is very serious. You can imagine my shock to see her show up here unannounced with a bullet lodged in her shoulder and blood everywhere."

"I know. I know," Jonathan said. He looked at the ground as they spoke. He was almost embarrassed. He felt like it was all his fault. He didn't know what to say.

"Well, thankfully you were there to bring her here. I will forever be in your debt. If you weren't there, I don't know what would have happened. I don't even want to think about what would have happened if you weren't there."

"I wish I could have done something… something more to protect her. I feel so terrible. I have this empty feeling in my stomach."

"What's really going on? Why are people after her? Is it because of you? Are they after you? Did you do something wrong?"

"It's not me that they're after… at least that's not what I think. I think they're after Jennifer. I think that they're after her for her research work."

"Her research work?"

"Yes," said Jonathan. "You know, her work in the states on advanced algorithms? The work on ciphers?"

"I guess I don't know as much about her life as I should. I haven't had much time to spend with her lately. I've been so busy with work myself."

"Oh… I'm sorry… I thought…"

"That's okay. I guess it probably looked like I would have known a lot more than I do," the doctor said. He re-crossed his legs, shifting from one side of the armchair to the other. Jonathan looked back out the window and seemingly got lost in another thought.

The evening's events were racing through his mind. For the first time in a long time, he actually feared for his life, and he actually cared enough to protect the life of someone he barely even knew. For two years he had beaten himself up over the death of his wife. For two long years he had suffered at the behest of his own personal demons.

"I'm sorry. I didn't mean to confuse things. I guess I'm just a little bit worried. I have a lot on my mind right now," Jonathan said. He sipped his coffee and looked at Mehmet.

"What are you going to do? What's your plan?" asked Mehmet. "These people that are after her… how are you going to help stop them?" It was clear that he was concerned as he eyed Jonathan with a twinge of suspicion. The doctor crossed his legs then re-crossed them over and over. It almost seemed like it was a nervous habit.

"I don't know right now. I really don't know what we're going to do. I think I have to make a phone call. Can you excuse me for a minute?"

"Sure, go ahead. There's an empty bedroom over there, at the other end of the apartment."

"Great. Be back in a few minutes."

Jonathan checked his watch – it was barely 9pm and the

sky still hadn't gone completely dark yet. That meant that it was 2pm in New York. He was still adjusting to the math in his head. He picked up his cell phone and dialed one of his only friends in New York.

"Blake?"

"Jon? Is that you? Where are you? What number is this?"

"Yeah, it's me. I'm overseas and I'm calling you from an international SIM. I'm in Istanbul right now."

"Istanbul?" Blake asked. "What the heck are you doing over there?"

"It's a work thing. Look, I need to ask you something. I need to ask you a favor. I know that I haven't been the best friend lately, what with all the drinking and all."

"Jon, I don't have any money to lend you. I really don't…"

"It's not that. I just… I need a favor from you."

"What is it? You know I'll help you with whatever I can."

"Are you still good friends with that reporter at the Times… what was his name again?"

"Ed Perkins?"

"Yeah, him. I haven't seen him in ages and I don't have his number anymore. I need you to get in touch with him for me… I've got a story that he's going to want to hear."

"Okay. I'll have him call you on this number."

"Great. Thanks, Blake," said Jonathan.

"Anytime."

9

The 245-foot superyacht came to dock in Istanbul's harbor. The massive vessel glistened on the water, serving as a reminder of the audacious wealth in the world. Boris Medviek adjusted his disguised prosthetic nose and faux facial hair in the mirror. It was a complete transformation. His thin and very pointy nose was replaced with a rounded and obtuse version that changed the profile of his face. The dark 1960's-style thick lenses added to an already complete alteration of his look. Once the superyacht secured itself in the harbor, Boris descended the ramp onto the docks in

Istanbul. His many passports afforded him the opportunity to travel the world in almost complete obscurity. Money could buy that for you. After spending years creating multiple identities for himself, he was armed with a treasure trove of personalities that he could assume at any given moment. To add to the allure, the yacht's registered owner was a Bearer Shares Corporation located in Panama, of which the obscurity and anonymity allowed him to travel virtually undetected around the world.

On shore, Boris climbed into the back of a black bulletproof Mercedes outfitted with the latest technology. The car hurried through the busy streets of Istanbul en route to a busy shopping district. He launched a smartphone app that housed a WiFi beacon. As the car traversed the streets, Boris used the app to locate the strongest WiFi signal he could find. The driver parked the car and Boris exited the vehicle with a black leather briefcase. At the café, Boris found a discreet corner inside where he could stay virtually unnoticed.

After getting set up, Boris ordered a coffee, plugged in the black USB cipher drive, and went to work. His fingers glided across the keyboard with the speed and efficiency of someone who knew exactly what he was doing. He could see his reflection in the glare of the black UNIX screens as he launched them to initiate his attack. First, he worked on ghosting his IP address through several proxies that created a roaming dynamic IP address. Anyone who wanted to even attempt to track him would have an enormous amount of difficulty doing so. The proxy servers allowed him just enough anonymity to not have his signal pinpointed. But still, he took precautions. He was careful beyond belief, because he knew what was at stake.

The first task – the easy one – was to locate Dr. Jennifer M. Cobalt and find out all the information he could on her. That part would be easy; he knew that. The second part would be to allocate the identities of field agents at the CIA, FBI, MI6, and NSA. He launched into a fury of typing, occasionally glancing up from under his glasses to survey his surroundings. Boris watched himself in the reflection of the UNIX browser as he entered the commands and responses were spit back out at him. He caught the glance of an occasional onlooker, but he sensed that he was fine. He was virtually untraceable. Again, he was a ghost. He watched the black USB cipher drive's LED lights flashing orange and green intermittently as ciphers were sent shooting across the depths of cyberspace. He smiled to himself as the commands were read, and databases were accessed.

He quickly cracked into Istanbul's healthcare system. He searched through the database using more UNIX commands against the primitively protected data on the other end. He knew that would be easy. The database was built on Oracle architecture, and he knew it like the back of his hand. His fingers continued flying across the keyboard as he listed records of the various hospitals and searched through the streaming data for records. No results. He couldn't find a hospital or medical center where a Dr. Jennifer Cobalt had been admitted. She had been smart. There were no check-ins at any of the area hospitals under that name. Could she have used an assumed name or an alias? No, he didn't think that would have happened.

His next browser screen launched into the Turkish telecom systems. He started with all the major telecoms and began hurling the ciphers across the Web. Within minutes, he had cracked the antiquated security through a brute-force attack. He used the doctor's Turkish cellphone number and immediately started searching the databases to find the right telecom that housed the phone number. Once he found it, his hands continued to fly across the screen, punching in more lines of code against the UNIX browsers until he had made his way into the telecom's graphical user interface. Once in, he had a much easier time scrolling through records in an easy-to-read format. He located all incoming and outgoing data for the phone number including text messages, GPS information, and phone calls. He saved the data, but used the GPS to pinpoint her exact location at that moment in time.

Once he had the coordinates, he picked up the phone and placed a call to Viktor.

"Da?" said the voice on the other end.

"It's Boris."

"Da. Yes, boss. I'm sorry, boss. I know that…"

Boris cut him off. "Get a pen. I need you to write down these coordinates."

"Okay, I'm ready."

Boris read off the exact GPS coordinates to Viktor over the phone and told him not to screw it up again. Once he was done with the phone call, he opened a final browser screen when someone bumped into his table. It was the server, who profusely apologized.

"Oh, özür dilerim," she said, apologizing.

And as if speaking perfect Turkish, Boris replied, "Bir şey değil." It was *no big deal*, but it was a big deal. She had interrupted his train of thought. She had broken his concentration. He was flustered, but he tried not to show it. But to Boris, it was an omen. It was a sign to stop what he was doing. He looked around carefully through dark glasses to see if anyone was watching. He couldn't be too careful. He was about to compromise the utmost valuable information in the world. He couldn't stay there any longer. It was too risky for him. He decided he would save it for another time. Something about the situation spooked him, and he left just as silently as he had arrived.

*****

Dr. Jennifer Cobalt opened her eyes late the next the morning. She had slept hard and heavy. The pain pills had severely sedated her. She tried to get her bearings and remember what had happened. Pain shot through her shoulder as she tried to get up. She briefly panicked. She looked over at the bandaged shoulder and remembered the gunshot. She looked around the empty bedroom and got herself up out of bed.

She staggered into the living room to find Mehmet and Jonathan there playing backgammon. They were laughing and having small talk when she walked into the room.

"Hello," Jonathan said.

"Hi."

He immediately got up from his seat and walked over to Jennifer. "Are you okay? How are you feeling? The shoulder…"

"It stings," she replied.

Mehmet got up, too, and walked over to give her a thorough checkup. "You know it's a good thing today is Saturday and I don't have rounds. You were able to get a good rest. How's the mobility? It will probably sting for a few weeks. You will have to keep your arm in a sling. Hang on, let me grab one for you." The doctor opened a closet, leafed through some supplies, and pulled out a sling for her shoulder. "Here, slip this on." He properly adjusted the device. "Now, how does that feel?"

"Okay. It still hurts, but I'll be okay. I can't thank you enough. Mehmet, I don't know what I would have done without you."

"It's okay."

They spoke in Turkish for a few minutes and Jonathan looked lost. He stood there and smiled, trying to get a grasp on what they were saying. Mehmet was certainly worried, that was for sure, but the specifics of the conversation went over his head.

"Mehmet," Jonathan said, once they were finished speaking. "Thank you as well. Thank you so much for helping us. But we shouldn't stay. We should really get moving." He looked at Jennifer with kind eyes. He had a look of empathy. He still felt incredibly responsible for the situation.

But before they were able to finish their conversation, there was a knock at the door.

"Are you expecting someone?" Jonathan asked. His tone was hushed, as if he the knock startled him. He was on edge. He quickly walked to the door and stood to the side of it. He motioned for Mehmet to come to the door and look through the peephole while Jonathan stood on the side.

Jonathan mouthed the words "Who is it?" to Mehmet, as he peered through the peephole.

"Delivery," Mehmet said, but only by moving his mouth and not saying a word. He shrugged his shoulders and started to unlock the door. As soon as the door was slightly ajar, and before he got a chance to unchain the link, it was kicked in. A man with a black ski mask on stormed in and shot three bullets square into the doctor who fell with a thud on the floor. The silenced gunshots echoed in Jonathan's mind, and he thought he was dreaming. He thought what he was looking at wasn't actually happening. He did the first thing he could think of – from behind the door, he punched the man as hard as he could. His fist erupted into a crunch of bone and skin, spattering blood across the apartment.

The gunmen fell to the floor and his gun fell a foot away from his hand. He tried to shake it off and crawl to the gun but Jonathan kicked him in the head, then in the stomach twice. On the second kick to the stomach, the gunman grabbed Jonathan's foot and twisted it, sending him crashing to the floor. Jennifer stood against the wall, watching in shock as the two men wrestled on the ground. Her friend, Mehmet, was dead, lying there in a pool of his own blood. She didn't feel like it was really happening. She didn't feel like any of it was real.

Jonathan and the gunmen wrestled, knocking down a pillar holding up a vase as they struggled on the ground. Jennifer didn't know what to do, but in a sudden fit of rage and anger she grabbed the first thing she could find – a silver pot on the dining room table – and slammed it into the head of the gunmen, knocking him out cold. Jonathan tried to get his bearings. He was looking at the gun but the wind was knocked out of him. He struggled to get up, and held his stomach.

"Oh my god, are you okay?" Jennifer stammered. What do we... I mean... what if..." She was stumbling for her words. She wasn't making any sense.

He stared into her pale blue eyes and said, "Run. We have to run right now." He grabbed Jennifer by her arm, and pulled her out of the apartment. The gunman was still knocked out cold.

"Grab the gun!" she yelled.

"Run!" Jonathan yelled back as he shot back into the apartment to take the gun. "No, not the elevator! The stairs! Run!"

They ran into the stairwell and glided down fifteen flights of stairs. Her arm still in a sling, Jennifer quickly hobbled, trying not to use the upper left side of her body. It made for an awkward descent down the stairs.

"Are you okay?" he asked as they reached the garage level.

"My shoulder is killing me. Do you still have the keys?" she asked. She was breathing heavily as they got to the car.

"Yes. Yes. They're here!"

"Let's go. Before he gets down here! Hurry up!" she yelled.

Jonathan fumbled with the keys. His nerves were frayed as he was trying to get the car door open.

"I'm shaking. I can't stop shaking…" he said.

"Drive!" she yelled. "Please… please… I don't want to die! Go! Please!"

Jonathan threw the car in gear and lurched out of the parking garage once the automatic door opened. He revved the engine and floored it down the steep embankment, screeching through twists and turns until they reached the bottom.

"How the hell did they find us?" he asked.

"I have no idea." She looked him in the eyes as he tried so desperately to evade the scene. He could see the look of terror wash over her face.

"They're tracking us. Somehow, they're tracking us. Quick. Where's your phone?"

"Here... It's right here..." She whipped out the phone from her purse and Jonathan grabbed it and took out the battery and the SIM card. He tossed the SIM card out the window as the car sped through the partially congested side streets.

"Yours, too. You should get rid of yours too."

"Yeah, you're right," he said back. His voice had changed into a monotonous sounding tone, as if he were speaking autonomously. Without looking, he did the same for his phone, and tossed the SIM card out the window.

"Now, how are we going to communicate with anyone?" she asked.

"We need to get new SIM cards – clean SIM cards. I suppose Turkey doesn't have pay-as-you-go phones, do they?"

"They're really not that up on technology just yet, but we could get new SIM cards. But, they usually do require identification. I have some friends in town who may be willing to help us out."

"No friends. We're going to do this on our own. I have to get to a phone and make some calls," he barked.

"Okay, okay… no need to yell anymore. I think we're in the clear," she said.

"In the clear? Are you kidding? We were just shot at TWICE in two days. I really think we need to figure this out. We need to get you to safety somehow. Otherwise, we're both toast."

10

In Washington DC, at a secret meeting called by the Director of the National Security Agency himself, the underground digital war room was lined with fresh-faced analysts paying close attention to Director Peter Edwards' speech. The enormous digital screen on the wall behind him had a map with a photo of Boris Medviek, the criminal mastermind who had orchestrated this worldwide network of coordinated attacks. The screen also displayed the names of his criminal network of cohorts that included names, locations, and additional intelligence on his likely targets.

"Okay, people, listen up. Here's what we have. Boris Medviek. Russian descent. 42 years old. Brilliant hacker. Current location is believed to be in Istanbul, Turkey. We've located a superyacht, which we believe to belong to him. He is a master of disguise people. We need to find him. This is our top priority. We believe that Medviek is working on infiltrating high-level government databases for the purposes of securing a list of agents in the field, which he plans to sell to the Saudis on the black market. We're also aware of recent infiltrations that we believe can be traced back to him. We believe that he's going to strike again very soon. This is top-level priority, people."

A security analyst by the name of Kate Jenkins, seated in the second row that lined the room from front to back, 7 per row, 6 rows deep, spoke up. "Sir, what if Boris already has the list with him? What if he's already infiltrated the databases? I found this," she said, punching some keys into the keyboard in front of her, then hitting a button to send the details to the screen up front. "I show infiltration points here, here, and here," she said referring to different databases across the NSA, CIA, and FBI.

"What's your name, analyst?"

"Jenkins, sir. Kate Jenkins."

"Well, Jenkins," said the Director, "Those security

points were breached, but no data was taken, however we can't be too cautious on this one. Let's double and triple-check all databases for security. I also want to gather a team of our best IT personnel to review security procedures for the data. He's somehow getting into our systems and we're unable to lock him out."

"Sir," Jenkins continued, "I've done some further analysis on this, and it seems as though it's a special kind of brute force attack."

"What's your background, Jenkins?"

"Advanced Cryptology and Applied Mathematics, sir. I did my thesis on advanced cryptography ciphers, and I have to say that the techniques being used to gain access look extremely advanced. We can see here, on the Air Traffic Control Systems' coordinated hack, that the brute force attack came in over a secured 1024-bit RSA key server. It's virtually impossible to hack a load-balanced server by brute force because they can normally withstand those types of attacks. This attack was either coordinated with several servers attacking all at once, or some other sophisticated method was used that I've never seen. But the fact that this type of attack has worked across the board tells us we're dealing with one very sophisticated cipher," said Jenkins.

Another analyst in the room named Geoff, seated in the

back row, also spoke up. "Sir, Geoff Steiner here," he said.

"Go ahead, Steiner," barked the Director.

"Sir, I've located some information that may be deemed useful here. We have a lab out of Arlington, Virginia called Advanced Biogenics, which was working on a technology for advanced ciphers. The team was led by this researcher," he said, punching some keys on the keyboard that brought up Jennifer's photo on the screen in front of them. "Her name is Dr. Jennifer M. Cobalt. She has a Harvard degree in Applied Mathematics and we have reason to believe, sir, that she created a new advanced algorithm that can hack a 2048-bit RSA key in less than 30 minutes."

The room grew silent after Steiner spoke. They looked at the screen with the doctor's photo on it, and the director took off his prescription lenses for a moment to wipe his eyes. "If this is true," said the Director, then we're in trouble, people. Do you realize what this means? This means that any institution, public or private, from financial to media, and everything in between, can be hacked. I want all of you to find out everything you can about Advanced Biogenics. I want to know everything about this doctor, and the team that worked on this project. I want to know how the hell Boris Medviek has this technology, if in fact he does."

"It all makes sense, sir," said Jenkins. "It's much more plausible to be able to launch a coordinated attack with technology like this. This would be impossible to do otherwise."

"Like I said, people, I want everything. I want absolutely everything we can rummage up. I want to know where she is, what she eats for breakfast, her first boyfriend's name. I want to know everything. And, we need eyes in the field. Let's get on this before it's too late."

The Director left the room and the analysts dispersed. Kate Jenkins and Geoff Steiner walked out of the room together, trailing the rest of the group.

"So what do you think of all of this?" asked Steiner.

"I think that if Medviek has this kind of technology, we're all screwed. It's going to be virtually impossible to stop it from leaking out, if it already hasn't. If this isn't a matter of national security, then I don't know what could be," Jenkins replied.

"So, this can't be a software-based cipher, can it?" asked Steiner.

"Well, I think it may be a hard-encoded cipher. It must be some new form of algorithm. I wouldn't know unless I could get a chance to see the research that went into it. But, most likely, it's a cipher sitting on a circuit. If that's the case, and there's multiple devices like this out there, then even if we get Medviek, we're not solving our problem."

"That's scary stuff," he said as they rounded the well-lit hallway enroute to their section in the underground spy station.

"I know," said Jenkins. "I did my master's dissertation on advanced ciphers. It seems hard to believe that someone could crack a 2048-bit RSA key. It was supposed to be virtually impossible. Well, at least not possible for years to come. I don't think this has anything to do with Moore's law. They've found some sort of key that can unlock these ciphers. It's like a master key of all ciphers. I have to sit down and think of it. I have to draft out my ideas," she said.

"Yeah, me too. Well, let's get to work," he replied.

"Okay. Let's regroup later today to review what we've found," said Jenkins as she rounded the hallway towards her office. The pair split up. It was clear they had a lot of work to do; they had a whole lot of work to do.

11

Jonathan Grace ran through the gears of the BMW as they sped through the city of Istanbul. He was at the wheel again, while Jennifer sat in the passenger seat, helpless with her arm in a sling, unable to drive the vehicle herself. Jonathan looked over at her sitting there helplessly, her pale blue eyes sparkling in the late morning sun of the city. The light Sunday traffic made navigating the streets much easier than normal. They whipped through cobblestone streets, along major highways, across a bridge over the Bosporus, and back onto more city streets.

"Where are we going?" she asked.

"Back to my hotel," he said.

"But it's not safe there. What if they're there waiting for us?" He could see the tense look on her face. She was stressed out and rightfully so. They had been through quite an ordeal, and it was taking a toll on her. She turned her gaze towards the city. "How do you even know where you're going?"

"I know it's through these streets, on this side of the Bosporus."

"Good memory," she said. She cracked a half-hearted smile.

"Thanks. But, what the hell are we going to do? We need to get out of here. This guy isn't going to stop until we're both dead." Jonathan felt the gun that was now between his legs. He hadn't held a gun in a long time and he knew that it was no toy. But, the fact that they had a gun made him feel much better. They were certainly going to need it. He held the brushed steel silencer of the gun in his hand for a moment and double-checked the safety. They were safe for the time being, but for how much longer? How much longer would it take for them to be found again? Were they tracking them via satellite? Did they have the license plate of their car?

"We have to ditch this car," he said. "Especially with

these gunshot holes in the windshield. We're going to be a pretty obvious target."

"I know. But, what are we going to do without a car? We need a car."

"We've got to find a different one," he said. "There's so much to do, but first things first. We need to get to the hotel, and we need to find that cipher drive."

"The cipher drive?" She looked at him with a puzzled expression. "How do you expect us to find that? It could be anywhere by now. It could be thousands of miles away," she said.

"We have to try. We don't have any other choice. It's why I'm here. That's the whole reason why I'm here. I didn't say anything earlier but I was sent here to find you because they thought you would know where the cipher drive is."

"They?" she asked. "Who the hell is they?" She shot an incredulous stare toward Jonathan.

"They… um… okay, I guess I should come clean," he said, as he spun the car around another bend in the meandering road that ran along the Bosporus.

"Spit it out." Jennifer charged. She wasn't in the mood for games.

"Okay, so here's the whole situation. I was paid to come

here and find the cipher drive. My client gave me your information. I was supposed to find you and locate the drive, then everything else happened, and now we're in this sticky situation."

"Sticky situation? You don't say." She laughed to herself, but it wasn't a funny laugh, it was more of a satirical laugh. She wasn't amused.

"Yeah… I guess… I'm having trouble finding the right words."

"I'll say."

"Okay," he continued, "Here's the situation. My life has been pretty screwed up the past couple of years. I guess this is no excuse, but this job was my ticket out of the hellhole that my life had become. There's a million dollars for me on the line."

"A million dollars? For what? For information leading to me?"

"No, no. That's not it," he cooed. He cranked the gears as he sped down the road, turning up another street, and driving away from the ocean and in towards the city and the hotel. "The million dollars is for bringing back the cipher drive."

"Look," Jennifer exclaimed, using my research to make a cipher drive didn't surprise me. I guess I just didn't foresee all of this happening. I wasn't thinking properly. I wasn't thinking at all when they coerced me into this. Advanced Biogenics – the lab that contracted my work – paid me a lot of money, too... In fact, it was so much money that I would never have to work another day in my life. It's not that I foresaw all this happening. And there's something else you should probably know."

"Okay? What is it?" Jonathan asked, quickly glancing at her as he drove the car through the city.

"There was a break-in at the lab; shortly after I had left. It was maybe a couple of weeks later, after I was gone. Someone broke in and ransacked the lab. My research was stolen; at least that's what they told me."

"Did they tell you exactly what had happened?" he asked.

"No. They kept me in the dark. But, I found out from a colleague of mine. She probably wasn't supposed to tell me, but she was a good friend."

"Was?" Jonathan asked.

"Yeah. Well, I haven't heard from her in ages. Her number is disconnected and the email bounces. When I tried to reach her at the lab, they told me she was no longer working there."

"But your research? Who stole it? What happened to

it?"

"First, you need to tell me who sent you here to find the cipher drive. Don't you think that would give us some clues?"

"I was sent by the Italian mob," he said, as he pulled the car up to the side of the hotel, and parked it on the street a block away from the entrance. He didn't want to park the vehicle right in front of the hotel and make their entrance obvious.

"Are you serious?"

"Yes. Well, it sounds more sinister than it is… I mean… I guess it is somewhat sinister come to think of it. Anyway, Don Cicerone is a client that's used my services in the past. It's been a couple of years since they had contacted me. I was a little bit surprised that they were willing to give me this job after not having had contact with them for so long. But, I think they felt sorry for me or something. I didn't really ask questions. I took the job and I'm here."

"I see. Well, now what? What's your brilliant plan?" she asked.

"We have to find the cipher drive. That's our only way out of this mess. Without it, we're toast. Whoever has it, wherever it is, whatever it takes, we need to find it. Do you have anything we can go on? Do you have any possible access to someone who might know about its whereabouts?"

"Maybe," she said. "Let me think about it. I could probably call Paul; he was in charge of another research unit at the lab. I could try to get in touch with him. Maybe he knows something. That would be my only option. But, why would you still want to go after this thing after all we've been through? Aren't you a little bit concerned for your life? I know I'm certainly concerned for my own life at the moment."

They sat there in the parked car looking at each other as they spoke about their circumstances. Jonathan couldn't help but feel attracted to her, even in that situation of heightened senses and nerves. He knew it was wrong on a professional level, but he couldn't help himself. He couldn't help the way that she made him feel; he just couldn't. And, she could sense his attraction; it was clear. She was attracted to him, too. After all, they had been through in such a short period of time, something somewhere along the way happened. It was something electric. He could just sense it in his bones and feel it in his heart. It was as raw and as real as any emotions that he had experienced in a long time.

"Yes, of course, I'm concerned," he said. "But, just know that I would never let anything bad happen to you.

You have to trust me on this."

"Why don't we just leave Istanbul all together? Why don't we just get out of here? It's safer that way. Don't you think so?" Jennifer asked. "If we just stay here, we're going to get in more trouble. I have money. We can leave. We can get out of here. Don't you think that's the best thing to do right about now? Sticking around isn't a good idea. I'm telling you this from experience."

"I don't know… I gave my word to Don Cicerone. I can't let him down. I mean it's my neck on the line. It's not just about collecting the million dollars. I made a promise, and with all of the promises that I've broken in my life, I wanted to make a clean start. I want to make things right. I need to make things right."

"Maybe you should speak to him, then. Maybe you should explain the situation to him. Tell him your life is in danger. Tell him our lives are in danger," she said.

"I spoke to him already. He told me that I might be in some danger; that you might be in some danger. I brushed it off. Now, I know to take things seriously. But things are different now. We'll be more prepared than we were before. No more mistakes. We're going to figure this whole thing out. I'm not sure how, but we are."

"Jonathan?"

"Yeah?"

"Do you remember in the news, that coordinated hacking effort that happened?"

"Yeah."

"The way they described that. The things that they said about it in the news piece leads me to believe that whoever did that is the person that has the cipher drive. Whoever orchestrated those attacks has what you're looking for," she said. "If we can somehow find out who did it, then we'll have something to go on so that we're not shooting around in the dark here."

"Okay, at least it's a start," he said.

"But I still think that we should just leave. I think we're taking a huge risk by sticking around," she said. Her sullen look was indicative of the mood.

"I don't want to run. Running isn't going to get us anywhere. I'm tired of feeling like I have to run away from things. I don't want to do that. I refuse to do that, in fact. No, we have to stay and figure this out. Look, we're intelligent people, we can put our heads together and sort this out if we really wanted to. Don't you think?"

"I suppose so. I guess maybe you're right," she said.

They got out of the car and casually walked into the hotel. Jonathan carefully scoped out the streets as they made their way in through the front door of the luxury all-suite hotel. His dark aviators made it easy for him to keep a careful eye on things while not revealing his paranoia. He tucked the gun into his black backpack that was now slung over his shoulder. He pulled it tightly to his chest as he slipped the hotel room key into the door and heard the customary double-chime before the green light lit and the door was unlocked.

Inside the hotel room, Jonathan looked through his phone. He thought about who he needed to call. He thought about who could actually help him in that situation. And, at that very moment, he knew what to do.

"I've got it," he said to Jennifer.

"What?" she asked. She looked at him with a puzzled expression.

"You call Paul from the lab, while I'm going to get on the phone with Ed Perkins, a friend of mine who works at the Times in New York."

"Okay, got it. But, first, I need to lie down. Do you mind if I get a bit of shuteye here? I'm exhausted," she said.

"Sure, I'll head down to the hotel bar so that I can give you a chance to rest," he replied. "I'm going to take my backpack with me. Don't open the door for anyone. I'll knock twice, then three times, then once – that's the code to open the door. 2-3-1," he said.

"Okay. I'll be okay. If I'm not awake, call my phone. You have the new number from the clean SIM card."

"Sounds good," he said. She had already slipped into the bed as he closed the door. He pulled his backpack tightly to his chest as he walked down the long hallway clad in a crimson red carpet. The dimly lit passage and red carpeting gave a certain elegant flair to the hotel.

When he got to the bar, he took a seat there among the busy crowd. It was high season and the hotel was pushing maximum occupancy. The crowd was that elitist jet-setting type, and he heard the gamut of languages from English to French, German, Italian, Japanese, and Russian. Istanbul was certainly a melting pot for an eclectic mixture of tourists from all regions of the world.

He pulled out his phone as he sat at the white stonewashed marble bar with its inlaid swirls of greys, blacks, and specks of silver. The lighting in the bar was just as perfect as it was throughout the rest of the hotel. He searched through his text messages for Ed's phone number, found it, and then dialed the number.

"Anything to drink?" asked the bartender.

"Whiskey sour, please," Jonathan replied.

"Hello?" said the voice on the other end of the phone.

"Ed?"

"Who is this?"

"It's Jonathan Grace."

"Jonathan? How the hell are you? Do you realize how early it is here?" he asked.

Jonathan hadn't thought about the time difference. He looked at his watch. It must have been around 4 o'clock in the morning. "Jesus, Ed, I'm really sorry. I didn't realize how early it was there."

"Where are you? Where are you calling from?"

"I'm in Istanbul."

"Why? For what?" he asked.

"On assignment. A job."

"Jesus, good for you. Glad to hear you're working. How's everything been since… well… since?"

"It's been okay. Thanks for asking. I still miss her every single day, but it's getting a little easier," Jonathan said. "It doesn't hurt as much anymore, but it's hard to forget something like that. It's hard to be reminded of the reality of my life each day I wake up. I'm sorry if that sounds so heavy."

"No, no. That's okay. I'm just glad to hear from you. I thought I would never speak to you again," said Ed.

"It's good to speak to you as well. I know that I've been

such a recluse, but I had to shut everyone out. I hope you understand."

"Yeah, it's okay, Jon. So, what's up? What's on your mind? I've got about an hour before I run into work so you're timing isn't too bad. I would have woken up in a half an hour regardless."

"I need to talk to you about something; something major," Jonathan said.

"Okay. I'm all ears," Ed said. His tone had suddenly changed to a much more serious one.

"You guys recently ran a story about a coordinated hacking effort. You know the one that affected the Air Traffic Control Systems, banks, water, and power. You know the one I'm talking about?"

"Yes... Yes, of course I do," he said.

"I may need some help from you. Look, I have reason to believe that the person who's orchestrating those attacks isn't a group. It isn't a bunch of hackers. It's just one person. One person who's using a little black cipher drive developed by a lab out of Arlington, Virginia called Advanced Biogenics."

"I've heard of them," Ed said.

Jonathan's whiskey sour landed in front of him as he chatted on the phone. He thanked the bartender and returned to his conversation.

"I'm in Istanbul right now with the lead researcher who created that cipher drive. I don't want to get too far into it over the phone, but there's some intense stuff going on right now. Someone is trying to kill us."

"What are you doing involved in that?"

"I was retained to find the cipher drive," Jonathan said.

"The cipher drive? The thing that's causing all of these hacks?" Ed asked, as if he wasn't entirely following the conversation. Maybe it was the early hour so Jonathan decided to explain it better.

"Okay, so here's the story. My job was to head out to Istanbul where the lead researcher presently is, and to find information that would lead to the cipher drive. I was essentially hired to get it back. Apparently, this device can crack 2048-bit RSA keys in under 30 minutes."

"2048-bit RSA keys? Jonathan, that's way over my head. Speak in layman's terms."

"Okay, I know it sounds confusing. Basically, that cipher drive can be used to hack into any known Website over any secure connection in the world. No matter what it is, this cipher drive can crack it. It's a tiny USB stick-sized device. The circuitry has been infused with the ciphers that can be used to do the hacking. I've no idea how it all works, but this is the information that I've been able to piece together," Jonathan said.

"Okay... you have my attention. What can I help with?"

"I need you to use your weight and your resources to help me find out who has the cipher drive. Dr. Cobalt... Jennifer, the lead researcher who I'm here with, said that there was a break-in at the lab not long after she departed. Someone must have broken in and stole that cipher drive. Is there any way you can help me to locate who it was?" Jonathan huffed into the phone. He stepped away from the crowded bar to speak in the corner of the room for a brief moment.

"I'll see what I can do. But, I can't promise you anything. I can't absolutely guarantee anything," said Ed. "However, I will tell you that this sounds like a story I can run with."

"Okay, great. I know you can't guarantee anything, but I would be forever grateful to you for whatever help you can provide. And, no stories until I can get this resolved. I don't want any of this information leaking out there to the public," Jonathan said.

"No problem. But, this is big. This is breaking news. I'm going to work my contacts when I get into the office today. Expect a call back from me. Can I reach you on this number?"

"Yes, this is my international SIM."

"Great. I'll call you this afternoon my time."

"Okay, thanks a lot," Jonathan said.

"You got it buddy," Ed replied.

Jonathan clicked the phone shut and walked back over to the bar. He sat down and nursed his whiskey sour. He looked down into the glass filled with that brown elixir that he had cherished so much not too long ago. Just a week prior he was washing his entire life down the bottom of a bottle. It had become a replacement for the lost love in his life. Alcohol had become the replacement for many things that he didn't have anymore. And, as he stared at the drink in his glass, he thought about how different his life and the world around him had become.

"Can I get you another?" asked the bartender as Jonathan polished off the first drink.

"Yes, please." He still couldn't say no to another drink. As much as he wanted to get right up and leave that bar, he couldn't.

"Great. Coming right up," replied the bartender.

"In town on business?" asked the man seated next to him.

"Yeah, something like that," Jonathan said. He looked at

the man warily. The blonde-haired business-suit-clad man looked harmless enough, but Jonathan knew he had to be guarded.

"I'm sorry… I guess I couldn't help but overhear some of your conversation. Are you a writer?" asked the man.

"No, I'm an investigator," Jonathan replied.

"I'm Adam. Adam Herschowitz," said the man. He reached out his hand to shake Jonathan's.

"Nice to meet you. Grace. Jonathan Grace."

"Sounds more like a secret agent's name," he said, chuckling to himself. "I'm assuming you're from the states?" he asked.

"Yes. New York. What about you?"

"Florida. I'm here on a company outing. Some merger we have going on. We're here to do some due diligence," he said.

"What do you do exactly?" Jonathan asked.

"I'm an attorney. Here, hang on a moment. Let me give you my card," Adam said. He pulled out a small gold business card holder, slipped out a card, and handed it over. Jonathan looked at it, with its silver-embossed lettering and expensive paper. Jonathan was impressed.

"That's some business card," Jonathan said, as he examined the card in his hand.

"Thanks," Adam said.

"You must be a pretty good attorney to have such fancy cards," Jonathan remarked, taking another swig of the whiskey sour.

"I'm good at what I do… certainly," he said modestly.

"What are you drinking?" Jonathan asked. "Let me buy you a drink. You drinking coffee?"

"It's an Irish Coffee. Sure, I'll get another one," he said.

Jonathan got the attention of the bartender who was busy running from one end of the bar to the other. "It's busy in here for a Sunday isn't it?" Jonathan asked.

"Sure is. Say, thanks for the drink. I really appreciate that," he said, as the Irish Coffee landed in front of him. He took a quick slurp and smiled. "Ah… now that's good. Have to keep up impressions and all," he added.

"Impressions?"

"Oh, yeah… you know, just in case the client shows up. Don't want them seeing me drinking at this early hour," he said.

"It's never too early to drink," Jonathan said. "At least, that's what I used to think." He polished off the first whiskey sour and started on his second one. So, do you just handle mergers and acquisitions?"

"You know, I used to be a civil litigator with my own

practice and the whole nine yards, but I'm now partner in this firm, and it's been about 10 years and running. I can't say that I have any complaints."

"That's pretty impressive. More so that your job brings you all the way out here," Jonathan said.

"I think it's you that's the one to envy. You look like you work for yourself with no one to answer to. Now that's something to admire. What's that like?"

"Well, it's not as glamorous as it may seem to you. The last couple of years have been rough, but I'm piecing things back together."

"But you found yourself on assignment in Istanbul of all places in the world. It can't be too bad right now for you, can it?" Adam asked.

Jonathan realized he was right. He realized that things were going much better in his life than they had for quite some time. Amidst all the anxiety and fear that the last 24 hours had brought him, that single conversation got him to realize just how much he did have to be thankful for. He looked at his drink, polished it off, and realized that he didn't need to have a third. He didn't need to go back down that rabbit hole again. It was as if a veil was being lifted off of his face. All of the bad the past couple of years had brought him was finally melting away. He looked around his environment and realized just how much he had to be thankful for. He knew that he would get through it. He knew that he would see things through, no matter what it took.

"You know, you're right," Jonathan said. "You're definitely right. Sometimes it takes another person to point that out to you, I suppose."

"Of course, anytime," Adam added. "Look, if you ever need anything, or you're ever in need of some legal advice, be sure to keep me in mind. It never hurts to network when you're away from the office. At least, that's my motto."

"Yes, absolutely. I'll do that," Jonathan remarked. "Be sure to do the same. Keep me in mind if you ever need any investigative work done back home in the states."

"Do you have a card with you?" Adam asked.

"Sure, here you go." Jonathan slid him a card.

"Great."

They smiled at one another. Adam left, and bid him goodbye. They promised they would see each other again at some point in the future, but regardless of whether they did or not, Jonathan was happy. He left the bar and headed back to the room to check on Jennifer. He was sure that she would be well rested by now.

12

Geoff Steiner knocked on Kate Jenkins's door at the underground NSA facility. The young analyst had uncovered a theory that he wanted to run by his colleague. Plus, she was easy on the eyes. He didn't mind speaking to her at any opportunity he had, and this was the perfect opportunity.

"Hey," he said, knocking lightly as he walked in.

"Hey yourself. What's up?" she asked, coyly.

"I think I've got something."

"What is it?"

"Okay, I was combing through some intelligence, and I

uncovered some chatter," he remarked.

"What kind of chatter? Sit down… please…" she motioned him to sit at one of the two black ergonomically-designed chairs in front of her glass and metal-framed desk.

"About the doctor – the researcher – Jennifer Cobalt."

"What did you find?" Jenkins was curious what her fellow analyst had unearthed so quickly.

"Okay, here it is," he said, as he took a seat in front of her desk. "I think there's a hit out on the doctor, and I think she's working with someone else. I have sources in the field that have conveyed information that the doctor has been shot, and that this man is the one who's after her," he said, spinning his tablet screen to show her an image of the man.

"Who is he?" she asked.

"Viktor Petrekov. Russian. Professional hit man. He's been on the NSA's radar forever."

"Not so professional is he?" she smiled. She was making light of a subject she knew she shouldn't be making light of.

"Well, no… but, that's not the point," he said.

"Who's the man the doctor's working with?"

"Jonathan Grace," Steiner said. "He seems to know her, and we think he's been aiding her escape the hit."

"We have to have some information on him. Do we

have a photo?"

"Yes. Here," he said, touching the screen a few times until Jonathan's photo appeared on the tablet. "This is him."

"We need to find him," Jenkins said. "We need to bring him in. Is he with her? Can we get a cell phone trace?" she asked.

"Working on that now, but there's a problem. Both the doctor's cell phone and Jonathan's cell phone went dark 24 hours ago. I'm certain they're working off of new SIM cards," he said.

"We need to find those numbers so that we can trace them. Access all the Turkish telecoms and comb through to see if we can find any phone numbers that would link either of them to any current contacts that they may have been in touch with. I want you to cross-reference every single phone number you can find. Comb through all the records. They're going to be calling contacts from a Turkish cell and when they do, I want those numbers traced," Jenkins replied.

"Okay, let's get them in right away. You know that this is top priority. You heard what the Director said, right?"

"Yeah, of course," he said. "Top priority. I'm on it."

"Good," Jenkins said.

"Okay see you later."

*****

Boris Medviek sat with his brother in the hot tub at the bow of his superyacht. The Eastern European supermodels graced their presence yet again. The music was pumping in the background, and they were all nodding their heads. Boris was about to pull off the job of the century. His brother knew it; he knew it. But no one else would know a damn thing. Not a single person would catch wind of what was going on until it was too late. Not a single person had the power or the resources to stop him.

They both looked out over the bow of the ship, onto the city of Istanbul. The mosques could be seen dotting the skyline as the boat cruised through the Bosporus. The rumbling of the engines was effortlessly masked with the sound of electronic music playing in the background. The ship's impeccable sound system had it wired for precision sound, easily dispersing any ambient noise. Speakers lined the decks, the cabins, and were located throughout the entire yacht. They bobbed their heads to the music as they cruised through the harbor, sipping on champagne. There was always reason to celebrate for Boris. He was so close to his goal. The mere thrill of the chase really got him going; the money was only secondary.

"What do you think, brother? Istanbul is beautiful, isn't it?" asked Dmitry.

"Yes, beautiful. Very much like these beauties," Boris said, nodding to the four beautiful women enjoying the hot tub with them.

"But we still have one loose end."

"What?"

"Viktor hasn't finished his job."

"I see," said Boris. "And why is that?"

"There have been some complications."

"Again?"

"Yes. I'm sorry. This time, we'll make sure it gets done properly."

"Look," Boris said, "I'm tired of these incompetent fools. If you want something done right, you have to do it yourself."

Dmitry looked at his brother, and didn't want to sour the mood. The girls were looking on, curious as to their conversation. "Drink up girls, drink up. There's plenty more where that came from," Dmitry said, trying to lighten the air. He raised his glass again and said cheers to the girls. They giggled and splashed their feet but Boris wasn't smiling.

"So, what's the solution?" asked Boris. "This was your

idea in the first place, and you can't even manage to pull off something this simple. It's a woman, dammit. How is this so complicated?" The supermodels looked on with curiosity, but they tried to remain aloof. They knew better than to meddle in Boris and Dmitry' s affairs.

"She has help."

"From who?"

"An American."

"What's his name?"

"Jonathan Grace or something."

"Who's he working for?" Boris was infuriated at this point. No amount of booze or distraction would appease him. He was about to pull off one of the most complicated jobs of his life, and he knew that all eyes would be on him. His stupid brother couldn't even manage to wipe a doctor clean off the map; he was useless.

"I don't know," Dmitry said. "I don't know who he's working for."

"Then what's he doing here?"

"We're trying to find that out now."

"Shit! This is unacceptable!" Boris yelled, spooking the girls.

"Girls, run along inside. I'll call you out in a few minutes," Dmitry said to them, shooing them away. The girls quickly got out of the hot tub and walked to the stern of the superyacht and into the interior.

"Do we have to do this ourselves?" Boris asked.

"No, no. Of course not. Let's give him one more chance."

"Where is he right now?"

"He's on his way to the port to meet with us."

"I don't want to meet with him. What's wrong with you?" Boris yelled at his brother, this time at the top of his lungs. "You're incompetent. You're no better than the Americans."

"We'll fix it. I promise brother," Dmitry barked back.

"You better fix it. Delivery date for the files is coming up, and we need to have all of the obstacles out of our way. Do you understand what this means? Is it getting inside that thick head of yours?"

"Yes, of course brother. Of course I do."

"Okay, then stop talking and start fixing," Boris yelled.

13

Jennifer was sobbing when Jonathan returned to the room. The uncontrollable tears were streaming from her face as she sat at the edge of the bed. He could hear her crying from just outside the door. He could hear her gasping for breath as she tried to fight back the tears. He knocked the secret knock, inserted his key, walked in, and sat down next to her, putting his arm around her. He allowed her to just sit there and cry. He didn't know what to say. It was a woman that he barely knew, but there he was trying to console her. Something about it just seemed right; something about it just seemed so normal to him.

"Hey. Please don't cry. You know it's all going to be okay," he said.

"You don't know that," she said, sniffling between words.

"Come on. I'm not going to let anything happen to you."

"How can you be so sure? How can you be so certain that someone isn't going to storm into this room at any moment and try to off us again? I can't even call my mother or anyone that I know. This is crazy. I don't know what to do. I barely slept while you were gone. All I could do was toss and turn around in this bed while my imagination got away from me."

Jonathan looked at her sitting next to him. Even in her worst hour, she was beautiful. Even with tears streaming down her face, she was the most beautiful woman he had ever met. He was such a sucker for a beautiful face. "Look, I know this is stressful. Believe me, I feel the same way. But, we need to formulate a plan. We need to be on the offense, not on the defense. All we've been doing is running. We need to plan."

"What plan? I can't deal with this pressure. I can't deal with the stress of someone trying to kill me; to kill us," she said, still sniffling between every few words. "I just want my life back. I just want things to go back to normal again. That's why I came back here. I just wanted to relax and not have all the stress and pressures of life back in the states."

"This has hardly anything to do with normal stresses and pressures, Jen. There is someone after you and me now because you have something they want," Jonathan said, pointing to her head. "They want what's in there. That's pretty clear. Why else would they be after you? Do you think it's a coincidence that all of this happened at once? I showed up and someone tried to kill you at the same time? The series of events that led us to where we are right now all started with that cipher drive. Whoever has that cipher drive wants to ensure that no one else can get their hands on that information."

She had finally stopped crying. "But, that doesn't make any sense," she said. "Why would they let me leave the lab? What would this have to do with that?"

"Don't you get it? Whoever broke into the lab is the person who has the cipher drive, not the people who hired you and let you leave. The person that has it now is the same person that wants you dead. You need to call your friend at that lab. You need to call…"

"Paul?"

"Yes, you need to call him," Jonathan still had his arm

around her as they spoke, and he pulled her near. He was expecting her to resist him, but she came closer to him, resting her head in the crevice of his neck and he felt electricity running up and down his body. He wanted so badly to kiss her, but he knew it wasn't the right time. He knew he couldn't take advantage of the moment, but before he could think about it again, she raised her head to meet his lips and gave him a gentle kiss that didn't last nearly as long as Jonathan would have liked.

"You're right," she said. "I have to stop being afraid, and pull myself together."

"That's the spirit," he said. He was still reeling from the gentle kiss but he tried to play it off. He tried to play it cool but was having a hard time. He didn't know if he should lean back in and give her another one. Before he could do anything, the moment had passed. She got up, grabbed her cell phone, and started searching for the number.

"What time is it on the east coast right now?"

"Early in the morning."

"Perfect," she said. She touched the screen on her phone and dialed the number, pressing the earpiece to her ear.

*****

Kate Jenkins and Geoff Steiner exited the plane at

Istanbul's Ataturk Airport and made their way through customs and immigration. They collected their bags and climbed into the rental car. They were on assignment from the NSA to find the doctor and secure the cipher drive. They needed to act fast before something else went wrong. Kate Jenkins navigated the rental car through the busy midweek traffic of Istanbul. The late morning congestion gave them a stark reminder of just how delimiting travel by car was in the city.

"This traffic is crazy," she said.

"I know."

"So what's first on the agenda?"

"We need to find the doctor," Steiner said.

"And Jonathan Grace?" she asked, rhetorically.

"Yeah. They're most likely together. We have a last known location at Istanbul's Le Hotel in Beşiktaş."

"Let's hit the hotel then," Jenkins cooed.

"That was two days ago," Steiner said. They could be long gone by now for all we know."

"Still, it's where we should start," she said. "At least we've got something. And, Medviek's superyacht is still in the harbor, so we need to get a pinpoint on his location."

"Okay, so we hit the hotel, then the harbor?" he asked.

"The hotel first and foremost. Not the harbor right

now. We don't want to spook them. We have no authority to do anything here right now. We still need to go through the proper channels," Jenkins said.

"Yeah, you're right. Okay, it's a plan. We should get setup at the hotel, then take it from there," Steiner said.

"Sounds good."

They fought their way through the traffic, and finally arrived at the hotel. They checked in and met with Erol, the manager of the hotel who allowed them access to the hotel's records.

"Can you tell me if Jonathan Grace is still checked in?" asked Jenkins, as they both stood over the hotel manager's shoulders watching him surf through the records. They knew the answer was no, but they decided to ask the question anyhow.

"No. Mr. Grace checked out two days ago," said Erol.

"Was there anyone else staying with him? Was he alone?" barked Steiner from behind him.

"He was with a woman. She was a tall blonde woman. Here, I can pull up the security footage," said the manager. He clicked around a few times and navigated to a black and white video feed of the doctor and Jonathan Grace checking out of the hotel. It had been over 48 hours. They could be long gone by now.

"Do you have any information on where they may have been going?" Jenkins asked.

"I'm sorry, but we don't collect that kind of information. As you can imagine, there's not much else that I can do for you." As expected from a luxury hotel in an international destination such as Istanbul, the hotel manager's English was nearly perfect.

"That's understandable. But, can you search the hotel records and see if you can locate a phone number for us? Possibly a local number?" asked Steiner.

"The only phone number we have is a New York based cellphone number. You can have the number. It's 212-555-7520," said the hotel manager.

"Okay," Jenkins said," We already have that number and it just goes to voicemail, but thank you anyway."

"No problem. Anything else I can do for you two?"

"No, that's about it."

Jenkins and Steiner left the hotel manager's office and headed for the rooftop terrace where they sat down to strategize on their next moves. The rooftop terrace had a sweeping view of the Bosporus, and they got lost in the beauty of it for a moment.

"Look at that view," Jenkins said.

"Yeah, pretty beautiful," Steiner replied.

"So, we need to track down every single lead we can in the city. This is Istanbul right? Doctor Cobalt has all sorts of family and friends in town. We should start there."

"Okay, I guess we're going to have our work cut out for us. It couldn't have been easier, could it? They couldn't have just still been in the hotel," he said.

"When is it ever that easy, Geoff?"

"I guess just once I wish it could be. Just once I wish things could just go according to plan and not have to work our butts off so hard."

"It's really not that much hard work," Jenkins said. "Just think about it and look where we are. We're in Istanbul. It's such a beautiful city," she added.

"Yeah, but we're not going to get to enjoy any of this beautiful city," Steiner said. He was being really sour.

"That's not true. Stop being so childish."

"We should probably contact Jennifer's family and friends."

"Agreed," she said. "Let's start on that just as soon as we enjoy a quick, but quiet lunch. I'm starving? Aren't you?"

"Yeah," he said. "Let's eat."

14

Boris Medviek took his place at another café in the heart of the city, just minutes away from his docked superyacht in Istanbul's harbor. His new disguise featured long blonde hair, green contacts, and hippie sunglasses. He was clad in board shorts, a tee shirt, and a pair of low-cut sneakers with no socks. He was about as casual-looking as he could be, and a stark contrast from his previous businesslike disguise. He had to be prepared for anything. He was certain that this much time in the city was going to garner attention, but he had no choice.

The moment had arrived where he would snake his way

into the NSA, FBI, MI6, and CIA databases. He was after those names. He wanted those names so badly he could just feel them in his grip. He was so close to finally getting that list; a list he would undoubtedly keep a copy of after it was passed on to the Saudi Sheik. He slipped open his laptop and the machine whirred to life. The metallic screaming machine was a top-of-the-line desktop replacement that had the computing power to handle any enterprise application. That computing power was necessary to help hurl the advanced ciphers located on the cipher drive he had now come to cherish so dearly. That one small piece of equipment meant absolute power. Without it, he couldn't accomplish his goals.

He looked around from beneath his sunglasses, as he parted his faux blonde hair to the side. He was clean-shaven this time with an entirely different prosthetic nose, which was joined by a prosthetic chin. His appearance was completely different than it was before. He truly was a master of disguise. His ability to slip in and out undetected in the physical world was rivaled only by what he could accomplish in the digital world. His fingers found their way flying across the keyboard as he launched his first UNIX browser and sent the commands hurling forward. His proxy servers provided him the anonymity he needed to complete the job. He was a ghost for all anyone knew; a completely undetectable ghost.

He launched separate UNIX browsers for the NSA, FBI, MI6, and CIA lists he was after. He was going for thousands of names; it would compromise the security of two of the world's superpowers. With those names, he would put all agents in the field at risk. With those names, he no longer had to fear the unknown. They would all be exposed. He would sell the names for a huge windfall, but he would also have the comfort of knowing where his enemies were. They couldn't hide anymore. They wouldn't be able to wreak as much havoc on his life and make him question his each and every move. He would be free to move about for a limited time by lifting their veil of anonymity. His mind raced a million-miles-a-minute as his fingers continued flying across the keys.

He slipped the black USB cipher drive into his laptop and watched the orange and green LED lights flash as the computer began to whir to life. He pictured the ciphers in his mind like missiles with the most powerful nuclear warheads aimed at their targets. That's what it felt like to him. He felt like he was at war, and he possessed the most powerful weapon in existence. That's what he had. That's what he was holding onto. He looked around the streets outside the café to ensure no one was trailing him. He had to make sure that no one was the wiser. He was a ghost, but he had to ensure he was a ghost. He couldn't rely on anyone else. He was on his own, on the streets alone, vulnerable, and exposed to people.

The anxiety fluttered through his mind like a hummingbird hovering over a flower. It was fleeting, however. The anxious thoughts passed, and he went back to hurling UNIX code at the screen. The four UNIX browsers were hard at work, each one of them sending through the brute-force ciphers to attack the systems. He knew it was risky attacking all four at once, so he had to roam his IP address. The changing proxies slowed things down but he had to be extra careful. His fingers continued to cruise across the keyboard as if he was a piano virtuoso playing his most precious concerto. A lifelong pursuit towards an inherent understanding of technology and the power of a single advanced piece of equipment was finally paying off. Those algorithms danced around in his mind as they danced around on the screen.

He was infiltrating their databases. He was in. One by one, he began searching for the information that he needed. One by one, he began generating his lists of data that he would then transfer through the infinite abyss of cyberspace and into his hands. One by one, each of those men and women in the field were becoming exposed. The names shot down the screen, each one of them appearing in long collated lists. Thousands of names were being generated. Thousands of poor men and women were having their identities exposed. The world wouldn't have to lie in wait anymore. That list was priceless.

As the information was downloaded and stored on his local laptop, he looked around again. Like always, he was expecting a sea of SWAT militia to show up with guns pointed at his head. But, like always, he was alone. He was secretly stealing a treasure trove of data and no one was the wiser. He looked around again as he was wrapping up his heist and almost couldn't believe he had gotten away with it. But, then again, he always got away with it. He was smarter than them, and at that moment, he felt the most maniacal wave of ecstasy that he had felt in recent years. He smiled to himself as he shut his laptop screen and walked towards his car awaiting his return on a nearby street.

He inconspicuously checked his surroundings as he made his way through the busy streets. As he slipped into the car, he directed the driver back to the docks where he would review his bounty and celebrate with his brother. The car meandered its way through the streets, the busy foot traffic slowing their progress as they neared the docks. That's when Boris heard the sirens. He could hear the wail of a local police car not far behind them. He looked out through the dark tinted windows to see the police car approaching quickly.

"Step on the gas!" he yelled at the driver.

The driver looked at him through the rearview mirror and could see that he was visibly upset. He punched the throttle down on the car and it lurched forward on the busy streets, nearly missing a group of pedestrians that were running across to the other side.

"Go faster! Faster!" Boris yelled. He looked back to see two more police vehicles approaching from the rear, just behind the first one. Three vehicles now made their way towards the bulletproof Mercedes. "How the hell did they find me? How the hell did they know?"

"I'm sorry sir. I'm going as fast as I can without killing anyone," the driver said sheepishly.

"I don't care who you kill. If you don't go faster I'm going to kill you," he said. He pulled out a gun and held it to the driver's head. "If you don't think I'm serious, then try me."

The driver's knuckles turned white as he slammed on the gas and threw the car violently forward through the traffic. He weaved through the crowded street, narrowly missing nearly every car along the way. Boris looked back to see the vehicles gaining, and was in a panic. He whipped out his phone and dialed his brother, Dmitry.

"They're following me!" he barked into the phone as Dmitry answered.

"Who? Who?" Dmitry asked.

"The police! What the hell went wrong?"

"I don't know. Did you get the list?"

"Yes! Of course, I got the list, but they're on me now. I've got to lose these people. Secure the yacht."

"Da. Okay, brother. Don't worry. We'll be ready over here," Dmitry said.

"Okay, I'm going now. Get the yacht out of the dock now."

"Will do, brother. Be safe. Hurry," he said.

Boris clicked the phone off, and looked back again. He was panicking. He was so confident he hadn't been spotted. How could they have found him? How could they have gotten wind of him? He was completely disguised. He thought he was a ghost. No matter, he thought, he had to lose the tail.

"Faster!" he yelled again at the driver. "Through here, cut through here," he yelled pointing to a side street.

"But I can't… the sidewalk… the people…"

Boris pointed the gun at the driver again. "Do it, now!"

The driver didn't need any more motivation than the gun in his face again. He dropped down a gear and the luxury sedan lurched forward and onto the sidewalk narrowly missing droves of people in the process. They sped along the sidewalk, doing their best to avoid the various obstacles along the way. In the process, they slammed into food vendors, smashed newspaper stands, and crashed into stopped bikes along the path. It was reckless, but Boris didn't care. He was only concerned with self-preservation. That was it. He didn't care about anything else. He had to get out of there with that list.

"Turn here! Here! Now!" he yelled again at the driver.

They made a sudden screeching right turn up a partially crowded side street, and Boris yelled at him again to hop the curb and avoid the congestion. He looked back at the cop cars that had stopped in the busy crowd as they made their getaway. He could see them back up in an attempt to hop the curb up the hill like they had done, but they were blocked by a large truck that had turned into the street behind them. Boris watched as the cops as they backtracked and turned down the street in an attempt to double around and block him in.

"Here! Here! Now, turn this way!" he yelled again, directing the driver as they continued to evade the police. All the while, Boris was watching his smartphone's navigational maps as they made their twists and turns. They meandered through more streets. His nerves grew more and more frayed by the minute. He could still hear the sirens as they whipped around another bend, nearly crashing into a building on the narrow corner, as they shot up the hill and into the city. He was safe for now. He sat back and breathed a sigh of relief.

"Keep driving. Don't stop! Let me out at the top of the hill by the taxi stand. Don't slow down. I want you to keep speeding. I'm going to open the door as you round the bend. Don't stop!" He was barking the orders at the driver who looked at him with cautious eyes as if to not upset him. He knew that one mistake could cost him his life. As they reached the top of the hill, the car screeched around the bend just as the police cars were finally seen coming up the hill.

As the car spun around the edge, Boris hopped out of the car, tumbling onto the sidewalk. The car door slammed and continued speeding off. Boris held tightly onto his green backpack containing the spoils of his heist, his trusted laptop, and the cipher drive. He gathered his composure, stood up, and slowly walked across the street and into a busy crowd of pedestrians. As the group of police cars came up the street, four of them were seen screeching around the corner close on the tail of the Mercedes that he was no longer a passenger in.

He wiped the perspiration off his forehead as he climbed into an awaiting taxi. He was safe for now. He barely made it by the skin of his teeth. He picked up his phone and dialed Dmitry.

"Brother?" said the voice on the other end.

"I'm safe," said Boris.

"Thank God," Dmitry said, exhaling a huge sigh of relief.

"Have you left the docks?"

"Yes."

"Police?"

"None."

"Okay, I'll meet you on the other side of the Bosporus at the Grand Bazaar."

We'll steam in that direction," Dmitry said.

"Okay. I'll see you there."

15

Jonathan Grace was having sensory overload. Walking through the passageways of the Grand Bazaar, Istanbul's largest indoor and outdoor market dating back to the Fifteenth century, mesmerized him. From the glittering jewels, to the opulently colored carpets, and the aromas of rich kebob meat roasting on opening fires, Jonathan felt like a kid in a candy store. The Grand Bazaar was a rare experience of culture that he had seldom been exposed to in his forty-something years of life.

"This place. It's… it's incredible," he said.

They walked slowly through the meandering

passageways of the Grand Bazaar, something Jennifer had done on countless occasions. "I know," she said. "I guess I've just gotten somewhat used to it. You know my father used to have a jewelry store here."

"What happened to it?"

"That was decades ago, now he just rents out the space. He's owned it forever, and buying something in here now is pricey. It's in very high demand, so he does well from his rentals."

"Like a little property tycoon isn't he?" he asked.

She laughed a bit to herself and Jonathan got butterflies. He hadn't remembered feeling that way about a girl in ages. "I guess so," she said. She smiled at him again. Her arm was no longer in a sling, but she was cautious not to give it too much movement.

"Hello?" she answered her phone and Jonathan stared at her. No one was supposed to have their numbers.

"Who is it?" Jonathan asked.

"Hang on a second, it's my mother," she said, and Jonathan breathed a sigh of relief.

"What did she say? Who's number did you write down?"

"That was strange. She told me that someone named Agent Jenkins called looking for me. She said it was urgent and that I needed to get back to her. How do they have my mom's phone number?"

"Well, she's related to you right? Of course they've probably somehow tracked down all of your family and friends," Jonathan added.

"I should call her, shouldn't I?"

"Yes."

"Okay," she said. She pushed the numbers into the screen of her phone and let it ring. The two of them stood in front of a grand carpet store that had the most richly colored carpets with the most vibrant crimson and purples Jonathan had ever seen on a rug.

"Hello? Is this Agent Jenkins?" she asked. Jonathan had to standby patiently while she spoke on the phone. He only caught one side of the conversation.

"This is Dr. Cobalt," she said. Then there was silence for a few minutes while she listened. "Okay… yeah… okay… yes… I understand… okay… sure… sounds good… bye."

"What the hell was that?" he asked.

She stood and stared at him for a few moments. "It's… it's… an NSA Agent. She wants to meet with us."

"When? Where?"

"Well, she's here… they're here… in Istanbul. She wants to meet this afternoon. At 3pm. She said she would call me back in an hour to coordinate an address."

"Did she say anything else? Did she tell you what it was about?" Jonathan asked.

"Loosely. She said it was better that we speak in person, but she said I would know what it was about."

"What do we do?"

"I don't know," she said.

"Do you think it's really an Agent from the NSA? What if it's someone else? What if it's a cover for the guy who's been trying to kill us?" he asked.

"I don't think so," she said. "I didn't get that feeling."

"You didn't get that feeling?" Jonathan half-heartedly chuckled to himself. "What do you mean you didn't get that feeling?"

"I don't know. It just sounded... I don't know... legitimate," she said softly. They started walking again, this time a bit slower as they spoke about what they had seen.

"Okay, well I guess I'll just take your word for it," he said.

"Good." She smiled at him and preened her hair. "Say, are you hungry? I've been starving. Do you want to grab a bite to eat?"

"Sure. What are you in the mood for?"

"Everything here is good," she said. "Do you like lamb

or chicken kebob? It's to die for here."

"Sounds good to me," he said.

*****

Boris Medviek walked casually along the city streets of Istanbul. He had just evaded capture by the skin of his teeth. Once things had calmed down, he made his way into another taxi. As the cabbie cruised down through the city streets, he could still hear the police sirens off in the distance, but he was safe; maybe he wasn't completely safe, but safe enough for the time being. He checked the GPS on his phone as the taxi made its way through the streets. And although he spoke near-perfect Turkish, he didn't look the part that day. His blonde surfer look certainly would raise some eyebrows if he spoke in Turkish.

"Do you speak English?" he asked the cab driver.

"Evet. A little bit."

"What's happening? Why are there so many police cars?" Boris asked. He knew exactly why, but he wanted to find out what the cab driver thought.

"I don't know. There are always police here," said the cab driver.

Boris smiled to himself a little bit. "Oh, okay."

"You, mister, where are you from? You not from Turkey."

"California. Los Angeles," Boris said. That was a boldface lie but he looked the part.

"Oh, I love very much California and Los Angeles. I hope one day to visit," he said in broken English.

"It's a beautiful place," replied Boris. But all he could think about was getting back on his yacht. All he could think about was how many countries would kill him right there just to gain access to the information he was carrying with him. The most valuable list in the world was in his possession.

"Yes, I hear very much things that it is beautiful. You are very lucky man. Why you come to Turkey for visit?" he asked in more broken English.

"For a vacation," Boris said.

"Oh, very good place to vacation."

"Can we go that way, over the bridge please?" Boris asked.

"Yes, of course," he said.

Jonathan was pointing in the direction towards the ocean, to the other side of the Bosporus where he would catch up with Dmitry and get back on board his yacht. But as they were rounding the corner and cruising swiftly down the ocean side road, he noticed a roadblock.

"What are those cars over there? Police cars?" asked

Boris.

"Yes. They block the bridge. They check ID. It okay. Do you have passport with you?" he asked.

"No, I forgot it at my hotel. Can we go a different direction?" Boris was in a panic. As they neared the police blockade, he tried his best to calmly tell him to take another route. However, the cab driver had his own ideas, and assured him it would be okay.

"No, no problem. It will not be problem. We explain. I will explain," he said.

"No," Boris said. "Turn around now. I don't want to go this direction. Take me in the other direction." But this time he said it with sinister determination, and he looked the cab driver directly in the eyes through the rearview mirror. If his eyes could have spoken, then would have said he was going to tear the cab driver's head off if he didn't turn around.

"But I cannot turn now. There is nowhere to turn. The police will understand." The car was stuck in the busy thoroughfare heading straight for the Bosporus Bridge. On the other side of that bridge was Boris's yacht, but between him and the yacht were the police.

He pulled out his gun and pointed it at the cab driver. "I didn't want to do this, but if you don't turn this taxi around right now, I'm going to kill you," he said in the most sinister tone.

"Please... please... no... I have children... please..."

But before Boris could say anything else, the cab driver put the car in park, opened the door, and started running. Boris was partially shocked by his actions. He got out of the backseat, hopped in the front, and spun the car around. The police cars, seeing the activity, started screaming. The cab driver ran towards them and yelled in Turkish for them to help, that a man with a gun was in his taxi.

Boris cursed underneath his breath. He never should have done that. He pushed the gas pedal down hard as the sirens started blaring behind him. He weaved in and out of the traffic in the other direction, narrowly missing several head-on collisions. He picked up his phone and called Dmitry again.

"Brother, where are you?" Dmitry asked.

"I'm stuck on this side. I need you to come back. The police are blocking the bridge. I can't cross."

"But we just arrived here. Police are all over the docks. We can't go back. You can't go there," Dmitry barked into the phone.

"Well, what the hell am I supposed to do?" Boris asked.

"I don't know brother. There is another route. You don't have to take the bridge. Check your GPS. We will wait here for you."

Boris was sick to his stomach. He was stuck on that side of the bridge and couldn't make it over. He should have just crossed, but he was certain they would have spotted him.

"Shit!"

"I don't know how you're going to get here brother. Just get here. We need to leave. There's too much heat here."

"Okay! Shit! I'm coming!"

Boris punched the directions into his phone and throttled it more as the cop cars creeped up behind him again. This time, he was behind the wheel. His safety was up to him, and only him. He had to evade them. He had to do whatever he could do to escape. His heart was racing and his mind was spinning. He had to get away. He had to.

He spun down a side street, shifting down a gear and redlining the engine as the tires of the yellow taxi screeched around the right corner. A woman screamed at him in Turkish as she tried to cross the street. He looked behind him to see the cops turning the corner as he swerved back to the left, this time narrowly missing a group of kids kicking a soccer ball across the street. He watched them curse at him through the rearview mirror, but all he could think about was escaping the cops.

The congested city streets made it difficult to evade the police, but it also made it equally difficult for them to chase him. He looked down at his navigation as he took the alternate route that added at least twenty more minutes to his journey, but he had no choice. He had to make his way around to the other side of the Bosporus and take the other bridge, then cross back over. He could still hear the sounds of the police sirens as he pushed the down on the gas and merged onto the highway. He could see the police not too far behind, and he began desperately weaving in and out of lanes, causing multiple accidents en route.

He was glad he was in Istanbul and not in the states. The silence in the air was golden to him. There was no helicopter making chase; no air support anywhere to be seen or heard. He pushed the throttle down harder, shifting into the fifth and final gear as he took the taxi to its limits. He continued weaving in and out until he hit the exit, screeching off the ramp and down a steep embankment where a red light awaited him. He slammed on the brakes hard as the taxi tried to stop just in the nick of time. Boris cursed the road and cursed the cars on it. Everyone was in his way.

His phone rang and he answered it. "Boris, brother, where are you?"

"I'm coming. These damn cops are still behind me."

"Shoot them," Dmitry yelled.

"I can't. I'm driving!" Boris yelled back.

"Okay, how long? How many minutes? We'll get the boat ready to leave."

"Fifteen minutes. Twenty minutes at the maximum," Boris barked into the phone.

"Okay, hurry. We're waiting."

Boris cursed into the phone and then hung up. He screeched through the red light, narrowly missing a head-on collision with a semi-truck. He couldn't stop. He couldn't slow down. He shot down streets following his navigation for what seemed like forever. Finally, he could see the docks. He could see his yacht. It wasn't far now. He was going to make it. He looked back and didn't see any cop cars or hear any sirens. He could breath a sigh of relief for now.

16

Jonathan and Jennifer got lost in the Grand Bazaar. With 5,000 shops and being the largest covered market in the world, it was easy to get lost in there. But they didn't mind. Had they not had the pressing life and death issues to tend to, they would have been perfectly fine leisurely combing the passageways of endless wares in that ancient market. But there were other things to do. They did, in fact, have much more pressing matters to attend to. But if you looked at their faces, the momentary emotional bliss that they both experienced had nothing to do with Boris Medviek, the cipher drive, or anything else for that matter. It had only to do with each other.

Something began to happen between those two. Something visceral was occurring. A bond was forming, and it was becoming a strong one at that. They were experiencing a rush of emotions that included fear and anxiety, but also included something else. They both couldn't describe it, but they could both sense that it was occurring; they knew that it was occurring. It was something that happened so rarely in life, that when it did, you just knew it. And they each knew it. They could feel it. They could sense the vibrational energy coming from one another, and it was powerful. But it also made them feel uneasy. There was a fear that came along with that strong emotional connection that was occurring.

As they passed one shop after another, various merchants stood in the passageways trying to coax would-be shoppers into purchasing their goods. They called out in English, Spanish, French, Italian, and German. They used whatever language they felt suited that particular passerby. And they were excellent at their trade. They were skilled at spotting the Americans and speaking English to them, or the Italians and speaking Italian to them. It was like watching an artist paint; they were masterful at it. It was inspiring to witness firsthand for both of them.

"I've always been so amazed at how these merchants just know that you speak English or Italian," said Jennifer.

"I've never seen anything like it," Jonathan replied. "How old is this place? It feels ancient?"

"It's said that it was constructed in 1461. Five and a half centuries ago," she said smiling.

"How do you not get lost in this place?"

"I know, it's pretty confusing," she said.

"I'll say so. Don't you think we should head over to the Aya Sofia?" Jonathan asked.

"Yes, it's in this direction. It's just a 15-minute walk from here," she cooed.

They walked through more passageways, each one connecting to another meandering route with hundreds upon hundreds of shops. Eventually, she led them towards the exit. They emerged into the city, which they traversed through the various little roads and staircases that led them towards the blue mosque, Aya Sophia. Agents Jenkins and Steiner were waiting for them outside of the entrance to the mosque. The agents immediately recognized the pair.

"Hi Jonathan, Dr. Cobalt," Jenkins said.

Steiner chimed in with a "Hello" as well.

"I'm Special Agent Jenkins, and this is Special Agent

Steiner. I can't tell you how happy we are to have tracked down the two of you," Jenkins said.

They walked towards a seating area outside the Aya Sophia, near a small group of outdoor eateries where they all sat down on low-slung benches. The area was a hotbed for tourists, and people milled about en masse, making the area much more crowded during this peak travel season.

"It's nice to meet you guys," Jonathan said.

"Hi," Jennifer said.

"I assume that you know why we're here?" asked Jenkins.

"Yes. I think so," Jennifer said while Jonathan looked on. She gave him a nervous glance.

"Mr. Grace, what's your connection with all of this? How did you come to meet Dr. Cobalt?" asked Steiner.

Jonathan looked at Jennifer and wasn't sure how to respond. He didn't want to let on that he was working for the Italians, but he also didn't want to leave information out that could cost him his life, or Jennifer her life.

"I'm here searching for something with her help. The cipher drive," Jonathan replied. It was as close to the truth as possible.

"But it's clear you two didn't know each other before your meeting here in Istanbul," Jenkins said. She wasn't asking, she was just saying.

"Yes," Jonathan said. "That's correct. We met here, in Istanbul."

"Who sent you?" Steiner asked.

Jonathan felt like he was being grilled. "Tell them," Jennifer said. "They're on our side."

"The Italians," Jonathan said.

Jenkins and Steiner both looked at each other as if that statement puzzled them. "The Italians?" they asked in unison.

"Yes, the Italians," Jonathan replied.

"Which Italians?" Jenkins asked.

"Why does it matter? I'm here, aren't I?" Jonathan asked. "I'm talking to you. I'm cooperating with you," he added.

"Look. We're not here to judge you or prosecute you. We're here for one reason and one reason only: to catch Boris Medviek. He's been on our radar for years now but has proven rather elusive. His criminal network extends into the far-reaching depths of the Russian underground. He has his hands in everything from arms dealing, to drugs, and human trafficking. So, I hope you can understand the severity of this situation. And, if you can't be upfront and honest with us, it's going to be that much harder to get this whole thing sorted out," Jenkins said. She was an expert negotiator.

Jennifer nudged Jonathan with her elbow, as if to tell him to let them know everything. Their lives were on the line. "Don Cicerone sent me."

The two agents looked at each other again with incredulity. "This just gets more and more twisted by the moment, doesn't it?" asked Steiner, speaking to Jenkins.

"Okay. Look, we'll get back to that part later," Jenkins said. "First off, I need you to tell me everything you know about the cipher drive you're after. I need to know everything. We need to find out what our exposure is here. This is looking like it's much worse than initially expected." She looked at Jennifer this time. "Dr. Cobalt, can you fill me in on the blanks here?"

"Yes," Jennifer said. "The cipher drive contains advanced cipher algorithms that I created. I was contracted by a lab in Arlington, Virginia called Advanced Biogenics."

"Okay, I think we know about your employment history there. But what type of ciphers specifically are these?" asked Jenkins, looking on with concern as if she was just about to hear some earth-shattering information.

"The kind of ciphers that can crack any RSA key, or any security on the Web for that matter. The ciphers are based on an advanced algorithm that I created. Traditionally, brute force algorithms work in one string where a device sends repeated attempts to in a relatively linear and consecutive manner to hack a portal or a server. My ciphers are different. I was able to come up with an algorithm that sits on a very different type of chipset. This chipset is much more advanced and acts more like a human brain."

"How so?" asked Jenkins?

"Okay, so in the human brain you know that there are billions of neurons. Each of these neurons – or nerve cells – is connected to other neurons by axons, which are the nerve fibers. The axons occur in synapses, the places where electrical impulses send signals from one neuron to another. These neurons are grouped in the brain based on what function they serve, which is why we have so many of them," Jennifer said.

The three looked on as Jennifer spoke, seemingly confused by the conversation that was going way over all of their heads. "So," she continued, "in this chipset there are thousands of processors that act like the neurons, thousands of equivalent memory modules that act as the axons, and tens of thousands of synapses, which act as the communication between the processors and memory units. It's because of this chipset that my advanced algorithms are much more highly effective because it's a multi-pronged attack, and not a lateral attack that would exist in traditional methods. It's that chipset, combined with the algorithms, that make this cipher drive highly lethal."

"When you say highly lethal, what are we talking about exactly?" asked Steiner.

"It's advanced enough to crack a 2048-bit RSA key in under 30 minutes," Jennifer said.

"That's impossible," Jenkins said.

"Not impossible. Very possible. In fact, very much so a reality," Jennifer cooed confidently.

"But present-day technology couldn't even hack a 1024-bit RSA key in under 7 months with some of the strongest computing power," Steiner said.

"I know," Jennifer said. "I know that."

The two agents looked at each other again with more incredulity. They couldn't believe what they were hearing. It was much worse than they had initially expected. "We have to get that cipher drive," Steiner said. "We believe that Medviek has accessed some critical databases from around the world. He has a list that we need to get back before it's too late."

"What list?" asked Jonathan.

"We can't divulge that information to you, but we're on

the same side here. We need that cipher drive," Jenkins said.

"Yes, I agree," Jonathan replied. Jennifer looked at him afterward as if to say that it was a stupid thing to say. She knew that his motivation for the cipher drive was money-related. She knew that it was the only reason why he was there. Yet, she somehow found herself being attracted to him. There was something about his damaged past that drew her in. She couldn't quite put her finger on it. She didn't know exactly what it was, but there was a spark there, something that seldom ever happened for her so she took very clear notice of it.

"So what's the plan?" Jennifer asked.

"Well, you have to understand that we're dealing with someone who's extremely sophisticated," Steiner said. He whipped out his laptop and started leafing through photos of Medviek. "This is Boris Medviek here. He's the head of a Russian crime syndicate with very deep pockets. He's very well connected and highly intelligent. He's also a master of disguise," he said as he showed different pictures of Medviek that looked like entirely different people.

"But that doesn't even look like the same person," Jonathan said.

"Yes, we're well aware. His disguises allow him to slip

through most places completely undetected," Jenkins said. The pair of agents made a great team. They fed off one another, one speaking first, then the other speaking next.

"So how do we find him?" Jennifer asked.

"Well, that part won't be that difficult. We're aware that his yacht is here in the area. In fact, it was parked in the harbor this morning. Presently, it's on the other side of the Bosporus. And, even though he's very cleverly shielded the true owner of the yacht through a Panamanian Bearer Shares Company, we've been able to track the ownership to him through a series of methods that I can't discuss with you all," Steiner said.

"What about the guy who shot me?" Jennifer asked. "What about that scum bag who shot at us, and almost killed us both, twice? What's being done about him?" Her faced turn red with anger as she was speaking. The thought of replaying those events in her mind infuriated her. She was angry that she was now the target of an obvious hit put out on her.

"That's Viktor Petrekov. He works for Medviek," Jenkins said.

"I don't understand why these people are after me. I don't understand why I'm the source of all of this. I didn't do anything aside from working on a project that I was contracted to do," Jennifer said.

"Yes, but you have the knowledge to recreate that. I think that's what they're afraid of," Steiner said.

"Yes, but without the chipset it means nothing. The reason why that cipher drive works is because it's sitting on that chipset," Jennifer said with an almost matter-of-fact look on her face.

"Well, they want you for what's up there then," Jenkins said pointing to Jennifer's head.

"Wanted for your brains," Jonathan said. He was trying to make light of the situation but no one laughed at his attempt at a joke.

"Well, so what are we going to do then?" Jonathan asked. "How do we get the cipher drive back, catch Medviek, and stop Petrekov from trying to kill us?"

Jenkins looked at the group. She was sure of the plan they had hatched, and she looked at the pair in the eyes, back and forth, as she explained in detail, just how they were going to go about it. "We do have a plan," she said. "This is what we're going to do…"

17

Boris Medviek climbed back onto his yacht after a lengthy battle to evade the Turkish police. But, he also returned to the glistening superyacht after having accomplished precisely what he had sought out to accomplish. He had the list. Not only did he have the list, but he still had the cipher drive. No one could take that away from him. No one else in the world held the power that he did as long as that cipher drive was in his possession. He could infiltrate any database, private or public, in the whole world. He could take what he wanted from whoever he wanted and no one could stop him. However, there was one thing that he still didn't have. There was one piece to the puzzle that still wasn't solved – the doctor.

When he arrived back on his yacht, his brother Dmitry greeted him like any other self-respecting Russian would: with a bottle of vodka. Dmitry poured two glasses of the triple-distilled and perfectly aged elixir into two ice-filled glasses. When he was finished, he handed the other glass to Boris and raised his own glass to meet his.

"Ura," Dmitry said, which meant cheers in Russian.

"What are you celebrating about?" Boris asked.

"We have the list now. Right brother? We can celebrate now. The money will be ours very soon," he said.

"I have the list, but I don't have the doctor. I want you to call Viktor. I want you to call him, then I want you to put me on the phone with him," Boris barked.

Dmitry walked over to grab his phone and returned to the wet bar at the stern of the boat where he had fixed his brother a drink. The shiny chrome and white marble finish of the bar glistened in the sun. But as Boris swiveled around the black leather barstool at the front of the bar, and his brother stood behind it, he shook his head. Dmitry dialed the number and handed the phone to Boris.

"Da?" said the voice on the other end.

"Viktor?" asked Boris.

"Da? Boris?"

"Yes."

"Hello boss," Viktor said.

"Hello? You idiot!" Boris yelled into the phone. "You greet me with hello? You are worthless! I pay you for a job and you can't even finish it!"

"I'm sorry. Really, I'm sorry. I will make it right."

"Where are you?" Boris barked the question into the phone.

"I'm here. I've located them. I am following them right now," Viktor said into the phone. Boris could hear the man breathing heavily. He knew that he was in a panic.

"Where are they?"

"They're in a car, on the other side of the Bosporus," Viktor said.

"Where are they going?"

"I don't know, boss, but I'm following them. They're with two others. What should I do?" he asked.

"Don't do anything!" Boris yelled back. "Don't do a single damn thing you idiot! You'll just screw it up again!"

"I won't. I'll make it right. I promise," Viktor said in his most apologetic tone.

"Listen," Boris yelled into the phone, "All I want from

you is to trail them. Follow them and let me know where they're going. When they stop, I want to know where they stop. Do you understand?"

"Yes, boss. Loud and clear," Viktor said.

Boris clicked the phone shut and stared at his brother, shaking his head again. He held the highball glass and jingled the ice cubes around by shaking the glass back and forth in his hand, and then he took one last swig of the vodka, polishing it off.

"What?" Dmitry asked. "What did he say?"

"Where did you find this idiot?" Boris asked. "He's following them. At least the idiot found them again. They can't be too smart if Viktor keeps finding them."

"What's the plan?" Dmitry asked.

"It's time to call Sheik Abdullah," Boris said. "It's time to unload this list."

"What about making a copy?" Dmitry asked.

"Let me worry about that. For now, we need to get him here for the exchange. We need to let him know that we have the list."

Dmitry grabbed the phone back and dialed the number for Sheik Abdullah, listened to the phone ringing, then handed the phone back to his brother. "Here you go," he said.

Boris grabbed the phone and listened to the tone as it rang on the other end. Sheik Abdullah promptly answered.

"Hello Boris," said the Sheik.

"Hello Sheik Abdullah," Boris said. His telephone demeanor was a 180-degree turn from that with which he spoke to Viktor.

"Has it been a week yet?" asked Boris. He smiled to himself. He knew he was early.

"You already have the list?" the Sheik asked.

"Did you not think I would get it so fast? Maybe not at all?" Boris asked.

"I had my doubts," the Sheik said slyly over the phone.

"Well, the list is ready. When can we meet?" Boris asked.

"How many names?"

"All of them," Boris said very slowly.

"You have all of the names?"

"3,486 field agents. That's three billion four-hundred eighty six million dollars," Boris said.

"Done," the Sheik said almost mater-of-factly. "I will be there in 36 hours."

"We're at the Istanbul port," Boris said.

"I expect that I will arrive by helicopter again, which won't be a problem, will it?" asked the Sheik

"No problem at all."

"Good, I'll see you in 36 hours," said the Sheik.

"See you then."

Boris clicked the phone shut and smiled at his brother. "Are you ready to make almost four billion dollars brother?"

Dmitry smiled. He finally got to see his brother happy. "I've been waiting for this moment for a long time," he said. "Glad to see you happy."

"I'll be happy when our little problem is taken care of," Boris said. "No more loose ends. Do you understand?"

"Yes. We'll take care of it. Don't worry... we'll take care of it."

*****

Jonathan and Jennifer sat in the back of the dark sedan helmed by Agent Steiner. In the front passenger seat was Agent Jenkins. They were en route to a rendezvous point in the heart of the city where they could be debriefed further on what they knew, and receive training for what was to come. Little did they know that the man who had failed twice to kill them was tailing not too far behind; little did they know what else was in store for them. They sat through the early afternoon traffic and quietly spoke to one another. They looked around at the scenery as they made their way past the front of the Aya Sophia and back towards the city center.

Looking out onto the ocean and the islands on the horizon beyond, Jonathan was still mesmerized by the beauty of Istanbul. "This place is stunning," he said to Jennifer.

"I'm glad you like it," she said smiling.

"What do you guys think of it here?" Jonathan asked the two agents in the front.

"Mesmerizing," said Agent Jenkins. "I've been here before and so has Agent Steiner, but it never ceases to amaze me. I've also seen other parts of the country. We were on assignment down in Antalya, which is a prime vacation spot in the country. You should see it there," Agent Jenkins said.

"I love Antalya. We used to take summer vacations there when I was a little girl," Jennifer said.

"So, where exactly are you guys staying?" Jonathan asked.

"A part of town called Nisantaş. Not too far from the first hotel you stayed in when you first arrived in town, Jonathan," said Agent Steiner. Jonathan looked at them with suspect. They apparently knew about that, too. He wondered what else they knew about that they weren't disclosing.

They arrived at the new hotel that Jonathan had checked into in the city center, and the two agents bid them farewell and told them they would meet again in the morning. Jonathan and Jennifer walked into the hotel and headed back towards the room. They both hadn't eaten and were feeling hungry, so they decided to head to the restaurant inside the hotel. They had checked in under assumed names – something that was easy to pull off in a city like Istanbul with a small bribe – so they felt relatively safe.

They sat down in the restaurant, which was virtually empty between the lunch and dinnertime rushes. "So, how do you feel about tomorrow? Are you ready?" Jonathan asked.

"To be honest, I'm really nervous," Jennifer said. "What about you?"

"I am, too, but I trust the agents. I don't think we can pull this off without their help."

"Yes, you're right. But what if something goes wrong? What if something really bad happens?" she asked.

"We'll deal with it. If something really bad happens, we'll just have to deal with it. There's nothing else we can do. If we don't get these guys, we'll have to watch our backs forever. I really don't want to have to be on the run, being chased by shadows, do you?" Jonathan asked.

"No, of course not."

"So, it's settled then."

"What's settled?" she asked. She picked up the menu and looked at it absentmindedly.

"That we're going to do it. That we're going to go through with it. We don't have any other choice."

"We always have choices, Jonathan," she cooed.

"I know that. What I meant is… oh never mind…"

"I know what you meant. You're trying to be supportive. You're trying to make me not worry. I appreciate it. I really do," she said. Her blonde hair fell in front of her eyes as she looked down at the menu. Jonathan wanted to reach over and brush it aside. He wanted to reach over and pull her face close and kiss her, but he didn't.

"Why did you really come back here? Why did you come all the way back to Istanbul? I know you grew up here, but it's so far away from your entire life the way you once knew it. It's so far away from Virginia. Don't you miss it at all? Don't you miss being back in the states?"

"Sure I do. But there were a lot of reasons why I came back. Aside from family, this is where I grew up. The states was home, but it was temporary, and I was burnt out. I was really burnt out. I worked my butt off for two years on this research project, and now it's come around to haunt me. Now, I'm running from my past," she said.

The waiter appeared and took their drink order. They decided on a bottle of white wine to start with, along with some appetizers. She ordered for the both of them. She spoke way too fast and her Turkish was impeccable. Most of the conversation was lost in translation for him, but he was happy she was there to order for the both of them.

"What do you mean 'running from your past'?" he asked. He looked at her as though he didn't understand.

"Jonathan, there's so much that… so much that you just don't know… that you just wouldn't really understand."

"Try me?" he said.

"Not now. Maybe another time. I really just don't want to get into all of this right now. I really don't…"

"I understand. It's been stressful. I know that. It will be okay. Things will get better. We'll get through this. We'll get through this together," he said with conviction. He reached over and grabbed her hand after the waiter poured the first couple of glasses of wine.

"I know," she said. "One way or another, we'll get through this." She squeezed his hand and it sent electricity running through his body. He couldn't profess just how he felt about her; he couldn't believe it himself. In such a short period of time, he had managed to develop these feelings for her. Now, he didn't want to leave her side. He didn't want to let her go. He couldn't let her go.

"Can I ask you something?"

"Sure," she said. "What is it?"

"I've been wanting to ask you this, but haven't really gotten around to it. I guess I didn't really find it appropriate before," he said, taking a big swig of the white wine in his glass.

"Yes?" she asked curiously.

"Why did you take that job? I mean, did you realize what you were actually doing? I know we talked about this, but when I was thinking about it in my mind, it just didn't make a whole lot of sense. Was it only for the money?"

"There were a lot of reasons. Money was one of them. Yes, I can't deny the fact that the money was very alluring. But algorithms and applied mathematics is a passion of mine. Imagine being paid really well for what you love doing in life. Could you imagine that?" she asked.

Yes, Jonathan certainly knew what that was like. He was living it at that moment. "Okay…"

"Imagine that for a moment. Wouldn't you jump at it? Wouldn't you jump at the opportunity to do that?" she asked.

"Yes, of course. Being here right now is exactly that, but didn't you think for a moment that what you were doing could be used to harm people? I mean, not directly, but indirectly. It's essentially a hacking device or a universal key that could give you access to any system in the world."

"Of course I thought about it, but it wasn't just my work, it was also the chipset. It was cutting edge stuff; the wave of the future. In 10 or 20 years from now, those chipsets are going to be the foundational CPUs used in artificial intelligence. I guess that even though I knew what I was doing might be used for some sinister purposes, that the allure of working on a project like that just drew me in. Does that make sense to you?" she asked. She took a big swig of her wine and polished it off before Jonathan could finish his, then she topped both glasses off.

Jonathan looked at her as her hair fell in front of her face again. That blonde hair that he wanted so badly to just move to the side away from her face. Her pale blue eyes locked with his soft brown eyes as soon as she looked up. She caught him looking at her with intent and it didn't bother her. There was something about him that drew her in, as well. She knew she was being sucked in. She didn't want to be; she didn't want to develop feelings for anyone else, but neither did he. They were both damaged, but in different ways.

"It makes sense… I guess… I just… I don't know. I was just curious, that's all. That's all it really was, just some curiosity," he said. But he wanted to say so much more to her. He wanted to tell her so many more things, but he didn't. He stopped short of doing that. But as the wine was polished off and a new bottle arrived along with the food, Jonathan was building up his nerve. He hadn't felt this nervous around a girl for years; not since his late wife. He didn't think he could feel anything for anyone again; he really didn't think he could.

"How's the food?" she asked.

"Incredible. Absolutely incredible. I never would have imagined how amazing everything could be here. And, you know, I do want to say one other thing," he added.

"What's that?" she asked with a sly smile on her face.

"I'm happy to be here. I'm actually very happy to be here. I know that we've been through a lot in a short period of time together, but I'm glad I took this job. I'm glad I had a chance to meet you."

"I am too," she said, smiling again, except this time it was a genuine smile. He could feel the sincerity in her voice. He could feel her actually meaning that, and it almost knocked him on his back. He was floored. He couldn't believe it. He couldn't believe the way he was feeling for her.

They continued their conversation over wine, and after the third bottle was completed and the dessert was devoured, they headed back to the hotel room. On the way, they held hands and walked side-by-side. He felt butterflies in his stomach, and she raised her eyebrows and preened her hair the entire way back to the hotel room. He could sense that she was actually flirting with him.

He opened the hotel room by slipping the key into the door and they fell onto the bed together. They locked in a heated embrace. He couldn't believe what was happening. He couldn't believe the way he was feeling. Her soft lips met his and he thought he had slipped into a dream. He wrapped his tongue around hers as they danced together to a silent sonnet in their mouths. It was wonderful. He couldn't have thought of a better feeling than that very moment. He flipped her over on the bed and was on top of her, kissing her. It was passionate and his mind was racing a million-miles-a-minute. He could feel his heart beating in the back of his throat as his tongue continued to lock with hers.

He broke the embrace momentarily and looked at her in her eyes. He was on top of her looking into her eyes and he held the back of her neck with his right hand, just behind her ear, and kissed her lips softly. He felt like he was back in high school again. Her lips were so perfect. Her eyes were so perfect. He became lost in another kiss. He felt like he could have kissed her for hours on end. There was nothing he wanted more than to kiss her like that, from the very first moment that he met her. Everything that had happened – everything that they had been through – had brought them to this very moment. And it was in this very moment that they became lost in one another. Two souls, who not too long ago were nothing but strangers, had intertwined their spirits with one another.

He held onto the back of her neck as he kissed her passionately. He still couldn't believe that it was happening. He pulled back again and she kissed the side of his face making her way to his ear. She breathed lightly into his ear and whispered, "I've wanted to kiss you like that for a long time now."

"Really?" he asked.

"Really," she said with the gentlest voice. She was like a little lioness lying there so perfectly. She really was perfect to him.

He embraced her in a kiss again. He wrapped his tongue around hers and pulled her face closer to his with his hand.

He had imagined this moment in his mind so many times over. He had pictured kissing her just like this, over and over again. It was so perfect; it was just as perfect as he had imagined. He wanted to freeze this moment in time and save it forever. He never wanted it to slip away. He never wanted her to slip away.

18

Boris Medviek sat in front of his laptop on his yacht, his fingers furiously gliding across the keyboard. He clicked the keys with purpose. He was on a mission. The glowing screen illuminated the dark living quarters of the superyacht. It was the middle of the night. As he sat there typing away, he realized what he was about to do. Amsterdam was just a test. He had tested the waters and he knew they were fine. He knew what he could do now. He knew what type of power he held in his hands. He was going to disrupt everything. He was going to bring the world's financial markets to a screeching halt.

He launched the UNIX browsers one by one, opening up infrastructure, financial, and communication portals. He was starting with Istanbul. He was going to cripple the city. Then it would be New York, Sydney, Los Angeles, and so on. They were on the hunt for him, and he was going to ensure that no one found him. He wouldn't allow them to interrupt his plans. He wasn't going to allow anything to come in the way of him and his goals. He continued typing furiously on the keyboard as the glowing screen spit back results to his commands. Line by line he hammered away. First, he was going to take out the power in Istanbul. Without power, they would have no means of communications. They would have no way to get him. He could do that. He could do more than that, in fact.

It was critical for him to use his satellite uplink on the superyacht. He needed the Internet connection to be constant. He couldn't allow himself to go into the city and be disconnected. Soon there would be no power, no Internet, and no means of communications in Istanbul. But his satellite uplink would be unaffected. He knew that and he knew the city was going to dive into complete chaos. After more clicks of the button, he sat back and watched the commands on the UNIX browsers spitting back one by one, and he waited. He waited until he had access to the

Istanbul power grid. It was just past 4am and there were 24 hours until his meeting with Sheik Abdullah. After that, he knew he could disappear.

A few more clicks of the keyboard, and he sat back upright in front of his glaring monitor. He was in. The primitive security made him laugh. They couldn't stop him, not without power or any other means of communications. He navigated through the Turkish infrastructure's Website and sent in the override codes. The power was going offline. While waiting for the system to generate more lines of code, he stepped outside onto the deck to feel the cool breeze of the evening air. The yacht was anchored at the dock and he looked out at the city and its lights. The yacht was self-sufficient, running on an onboard power generator. He was fueled up and ready for the crisis. He waited out on the deck until the city's lights went out.

As he looked out onto the horizon, he saw the streetlights going off one by one. Little by little, each section of the city lost power as the grid came offline. He knew that there would be panic, but it wouldn't happen right away. He ran back inside to his laptop and took his seat in front of it. He watched as the commands streamed down the screen as his overrides for the power grid went into effect. He would only have a small window, but that's all he would need. He only needed one short day and he was going to disrupt this city and others by any means necessary. He continued with his task as his fingers glided across the screen. He would now interrupt the telecom companies in Istanbul. Once he flipped the switch, all home phones and cell phones would stop working. Communications would be gone and he would be a ghost.

He acted fast. He suspended the power grid shut off to the major telecoms by furiously typing in the UNIX browser screen. He needed to gain access and implant a virus before all power was gone. He slammed violently on the keys, his fingers moving with incredible quickness. He was analyzing, testing, debugging, and sending data at a lightning rate. He felt like he was part of the machine. He felt like he was one with the technology. The maniacal thoughts swirled through his head as he looked out at the partially-lit city through the superyacht's vast banks of windows and he smiled to himself. He watched as he gained access to the telecoms and initiated an all-out-attack with more pounding of the keys. The sun was still hours from rising, and he still had so much work to do.

His next stop was Air Traffic Control in the United States. He launched another UNIX browser and wormed his way into the system. He violated their heavily-protected databases in a matter of minutes. What he reveled in was the fact that all of the world's information was connected to the Web; all of that information was very accessible to him. He had his fingers on the pulse of data. Private information was no longer private; that data was no longer protected by the virtual barriers that once seemed so secure. He accessed the system and began changing the courses for two airplanes flying across the US. He was going to make them collide and they wouldn't know the difference. He quickly hacked the systems and changed the courses and elevations of the planes by a few degrees. Next, he hacked into the planes themselves and set a virus to automatically shut down radar. They wouldn't know what hit them until it was too late.

Finally, he was back into the financial markets. He reviewed his short sales of stocks on the airlines and he knew that a major catastrophe in the air would send airline stocks crashing down along with the major markets throughout the world. When they got wind that it was a terrorist attack, those shares would tank and he would make millions more on just a careless stock play. He smiled to himself as his brother appeared next to him.

"What's the progress?" asked Dmitry.

"The plan is set. Everything is in place," Boris said.

"What about the power?" he asked.

"Look out onto the city," Boris said, pointing towards the windows. "Do you see most of the lights are off?"

Dmitry smiled. "Yes."

Boris smiled back at him. "There's your answer," he said.

*****

"Good morning sleepy head," Jonathan said, yawning awake. The daylight was streaming in through the windows.

"What time is it?" Jennifer asked.

He looked at the alarm clock on the bedside table and noticed it was off. *That's strange.* He looked at his watch to check the time. "It's 9 o'clock in the morning," he said. He yawned and came in for a hug and a kiss.

"It's too early," she said.

Jonathan smiled. They still had an hour before they were set to leave. He picked up the remote control for the television, but it wouldn't turn on. "That's strange," he said.

"What?"

"The TV doesn't work and the alarm is off."

"Maybe something's wrong with the power," she said, as she stretched and yawned awake.

"Maybe," he said. He looked at his cellphone and saw that he didn't have service. "And no service on the cellphone."

"Really?" she asked. She sat up immediately on the bed and reached for her own cellphone.

"Me too," she remarked.

"That's strange. That's really strange. I'm going to head downstairs and see what the problem is."

"Okay," she replied.

Jonathan got dressed and walked over to the elevator. No power. The lights were off in the hallway and the elevators weren't working. He took the stairs and ran down the eight flights until he reached the lobby, which was crowded with people. He looked around and saw that they were swarming the front desk.

"What's going on?" Jonathan asked a man in the lobby.

"Power is out," he said. "It's been out all morning."

"Did they say when it will come back on?" Jonathan asked.

"It's not just the hotel. It's the entire city."

"The whole city is without power right now?"

"Yes. That's what it seems like," said the man.

Jonathan realized that without power, they couldn't do anything. They were supposed to meet up with the agents in the lobby at 10am, but they would have no way of contacting them without cellphone service.

"Say," asked Jonathan to the man.

"Yes?"

"Do you have cellphone service?"

"No. Cellphones are out, too. Even the landlines aren't working. Everything has been cut off."

"That's so strange," Jonathan said. "Do they know what's going on?"

"They're as lost as we are. They have no clue," said the man.

"Okay, well, thanks," Jonathan said.

He ran back into the stairwell, shot up the eight flights of steps, and slipped the hotel key into the door. It wouldn't work so he knocked. He rushed back into the room completely out of breath.

"Hey," she said.

"Hey," Jonathan said, panting. "Power is out. So is all cellphone service."

"What?"

"Yeah, seriously. I don't know what's going on but it doesn't look good at all. I don't like this one bit," he said.

"It's Medviek," she said, staring out the window. "What the heck is going to be next? Jonathan, this is crazy."

"I know. I know," he said.

"We have to go. We have to meet Jenkins and Steiner.

They should be here any minute."

"Okay," he said.

They left the hotel room, but then realized they wouldn't be able to get back in later. They walked down the flight of stairs that was now congested with other hotel guests all doing the same thing. They reached the lobby and it was even more chaotic than just a few minutes ago when Jonathan had left it.

"Wow, this is crazy," she said.

They walked outside and heard all the cars honking. All the traffic lights were out and it was complete pandemonium on the streets. Luckily, Agent Jenkins and Steiner were already outside waiting in front of the hotel.

"Hey," Jonathan said as they closed the door and climbed into the backseat of the car.

"Hey," they said in unison.

"You guys see all this?" Jonathan asked.

"Yeah, it was a hell of a struggle getting here, let me tell you that much," Steiner said, who was in the driver's seat this time.

"You guys okay?" Jenkins asked.

"Yes," Jennifer added. "Just a little bit peeved. Are we still going to be able to do what we planned on doing today?"

"Yes. Nothing has changed," Jenkins said. "Power should be back at some point soon. We just have to push forward with the plans."

"Great," Jonathan said.

Steiner fought the traffic through the city, honking the horn in unison with dozens of other cars. They made their way to the outskirts of the city to an old abandoned building. When they arrived there, Jonathan and Jennifer looked at one another as if uneasy with the whole situation.

"Is this place safe?" Jennifer asked.

"Yes, it looks abandoned, but don't worry," Jenkins said.

They pulled into a garage that was part of the building. Steiner reached over and punched a keypad and an old steel garage door opened. The door opened, and he drove the car through, winding his way down a garage that went down several levels.

"What is this place?" Jonathan asked.

"You'll see. We're almost there. We'll get you all setup as soon as we get down there," Jenkins said.

"If the power is out, how is there power here?" Jonathan asked.

"The building has its own generators," Jenkins said.

"Well, that's a relief," Jennifer said.

"Yes, we're completely ready for any situation here. The whole city or country may be without power, but we're fine. We're up and running here. And, there's a satellite uplink down there. Access to news, Internet, and everything else is going to be available," Jenkins said.

"You guys are certainly prepared, aren't you?" Jonathan asked.

The two agents smiled in the front seat. They knew they had their work cut out for them, but they were going to make progress little by little, no matter what it took. Still, they were glad the two took notice of their efforts.

"This was all here before any of this happened. It was created by a joint security taskforce between the American and Turkish governments. We'll explain more when we get inside. For the time being, get prepared to work," Jenkins said.

The two agents nodded at one another as if they had said the right things at the right time. Jonathan and Jennifer looked at one another as if pleased by the turn of events. They realized that they were going to be much more prepared than they had initially thought.

19

A tragic accident today in the sky – Two planes collided over the Atlantic Ocean off the coast of Long Island, New York ... 621 Passengers are feared to be lost. In other news, massive power outages in Istanbul and New York City have crippled services and communications. Authorities are searching for a motive in the attacks. Financial markets have been sent plummeting today. The Dow, S&P 500, and the NASDAQ were in a free-fall before trading was halted in New York on news that terrorist attacks have been leading to the recent problems reported in major cities around the world. Air Traffic Control Systems in the United States and other parts of the world have been infiltrated in what the police are calling 'another sophisticated cyber attack.'

Jonathan and Jennifer watched the TV screen in the heavily-fortified underground bunker. They stared at it in disbelief. Agents Steiner and Jenkins stood in the room where a slew of joint security personnel were present to debrief the doctor and the detective.

"Mr. Grace, Dr. Cobalt, it's nice to meet you. I'm NSA Director Peter Edwards." The dark-haired colonel reached out his hand and greeted the two civilians. "I'm sorry you've had to hear the news here first."

"This is terrible," Jonathan said.

"Oh my God," Jennifer followed with a hand over her mouth. "All of those people. Was this…"

"Yes, it was Medviek. We have reason to believe that he infiltrated several secure systems early this morning local time," said the Director.

"This is absolutely terrible," Jenkins said. Steiner nodded in agreement. "We really have to catch this bastard."

"He's proven to be very elusive," the Director said. He looked at everyone in the room as he spoke. "But, it's now or never. He has that list and we need to make sure the data isn't passed off. We know he's here on the yacht in port. We need to infiltrate that yacht now and we need to do it fast, but we need to do it with tact. We know that he's most likely planned for whatever contingencies he's setup to evade us. We don't want to capture him then find that the list or the cipher drive has changed hands."

"That's why we need to send in these two," Steiner said.

"What's our angle?" asked the Director.

"Jenkins and I have been discussing that. We have a plan."

"Well, let's get to work before more bad stuff happens. We need to get that cipher drive and we need to get it fast. Have you debriefed Dr. Cobalt yet on everything she knows?" asked the Director.

"Not formally," Jenkins said.

"Okay, let's get setup in the room. I want to know everything and we don't have much time," said the Director.

Jonathan and Jennifer looked at one another again. They wondered if they had made the right decision. They wondered what would happen to them if they didn't cooperate, and worse, what would happen if they did cooperate and something went wrong. They gave each other nervous glances as they were led to an interrogation room for debriefing. They had more vested in each other than ever before.

"Please take a seat," Jenkins said. She pointed to the two chairs that were directly opposite one another at a small table in a room with a single one-way mirror. The Director of the NSA sat in an observatory room where he could listen and watch from the outside looking in.

"I'm going to start the video camera here," Steiner said as he made his way over to a video camera that had been positioned at the side of the table with a full view of all four parties involved in the interrogation.

"I don't understand why we need to be interrogated," Jonathan said. "We told you that we would cooperate."

"Detective Grace... err... Mr. Grace, you have to understand that this is now a matter of national security. More than just your lives are at stake here. As you saw and heard on the news update with what's going on around the world, many lives are at risk," Steiner said still standing after having turned on the camera to record.

"I understand. I guess this has gotten blown up much larger than it started out to be," Jonathan said.

"You can say that again. For the record, could you please both state your names?" Jenkins said.

"Jonathan Grace."

"Jennifer Cobalt."

"Thank you, Mr Grace, could you please tell me how

you came about meeting Ms. Cobalt for the record?" Jenkins asked.

Jonathan looked at Jennifer with a certain degree of concern. She nodded her head at him as if to tell him it was okay, and that he should speak freely.

"I hadn't met Ms. Cobalt before I arrived in Istanbul. We met only a short while ago, but it feels like since we met, we've been to hell and back together."

"And why did you come to Istanbul?" Jenkins asked.

"I was supposed to retrieve the cipher drive."

"And you were told that Ms. Cobalt had it?"

"Not exactly," Jonathan said.

"Okay? What were you told exactly and by whom?" Jenkins asked. She stood up this time and paced the room. She looked agitated. Something was bothering her. Jonathan and Jennifer both watched her pacing back and forth.

"Is something wrong?" Jonathan asked.

"Just answer the question," Steiner said, who's once pleasant demeanor had now turned sour.

"Well, I was hired to find the cipher drive for a client."

"By whom?" Jenkins asked.

"Joe Cicerone," Jonathan said, looking down at the table as if he was embarrassed to say it.

"Don Cicerone of the Italian Mob Family?"

"Yes."

"What's your connection to their syndicated criminal network?" Jenkins asked.

Jonathan certainly felt like he was being interrogated. He just wanted to run out of that room as fast as he could, grab Jennifer by the arm, and never look back. "What do you mean?"

"Why would an Italian Mob Boss want to hire you to do a job for them?"

"I've done work for them in the past," Jonathan said, mawkishly.

"What kind of work?" Steiner asked this time.

"Investigative work."

"What *kind of investigative work?*" It was Jenkins asking this time. Jonathan wished just one of them would talk instead of having them alternating the questions. Plus, Jenkins was still pacing the room, which further put Jonathan on edge.

"The kind of work that involves finding people or uncovering dirt on people. I'm an investigator," he said. "That's my job. That's what I do."

"We know your background Mr. Grace. We know the type of work you've done, but we also know that you haven't taken on new business in over two years. So, out of the blue, you get a call from Don Cicerone and you decide to take the job? Something doesn't add up here." Jenkins said, her face turning red.

"Why am I feeling like I've done something wrong here?" Jonathan asked. He looked at Jennifer nervously.

"Answer the question," Steiner said.

"What was the question?"

"Why did you take the job after two years on the lam?"

"Why do I have to even answer that question? What does that even have to do with anything? I don't get it," Jonathan said. "I didn't do anything wrong here. We're wasting our time on this when we should be going after Medviek."

"We'll get to that Mr. Grace. For the time being, we need you to cooperate with us. We're not asking you; we're telling you," Jenkins said.

It was strange watching them turn from two mild-mannered individuals into irate government agents. But, Jonathan did as he was told. He answered their questions to the best of his knowledge. Jennifer reached under the table and squeezed his hand out of sight, as if to tell him it was going to be okay.

"Fine. So you want to know why I took the job?"

"Yes," Jenkins said, still pacing the room. Jonathan's eyes followed her back and forth, as she walked from one end of the room to the other.

"I needed the money."

"You needed the money?" Jenkins asked.

"Yeah. I needed the money."

"But, why would Don Cicerone call you of all people? Especially considering you hadn't had contact with him in over two years. Why you Mr. Grace?"

"I don't know. Why don't you ask him that question," Jonathan said, feeling combative all of a sudden.

"Please, Mr. Grace. We need you to cooperate with us," Steiner said. They were playing some weird rendition of good cop, bad cop for no apparent reason.

"I am cooperating."

"It doesn't sound like it," Jenkins barked back.

"What else do you want me to say? What else do you want me to tell you? You want to know about the alcoholism? You want to know about how shitty my life has been these past two years? You want to know why I contemplated suicide dozens of times after my wife died? What do you want to know? What?" Jonathan was done being a lap dog; he was tired of being verbally abused and feeling like he had done something wrong. All he wanted to do was do the job he was paid for until he had met Jennifer. All he wanted to do now was make sure she was safe.

Jenkins sat back down after that verbal tirade by Jonathan. She hadn't realized the severity of his situation. She was an expert at analyzing body language. She could tell when someone was lying to her. She sat down and stared at Jonathan. She was going to watch him like a hawk.

"I'm sorry about your ex-wife, Mr. Grace," Jenkins said. "I really am."

Jonathan looked down at the table, and quickly glanced at Jennifer. Was she going to dislike him now that he had blown up at the two agents? He didn't want her thinking poorly of him.

"I know. It's okay. I'm sorry that I yelled," Jonathan said.

Agent Jenkins put her hands in front of her and clasped them together on the table underneath the white fluorescent lights of the room. Jonathan felt like the room was sucking the energy out of him.

"When was the last time you took a job for Don Cicerone?" she asked.

"A little over two years ago. Before my wife passed."

"What type of job was it?"

"Missing person," Jonathan said.

"Which person?" Jenkins asked.

"I don't see why I have to answer these questions," Jonathan replied.

"Please just answer the question," Steiner said.

"Jonathan, please… the sooner we finish this, the sooner we can get out of here," Jennifer said. She looked at him in the eyes and it made his heart melt.

"Tyler Walker."

"The mob informant that turned state's evidence?"

"Yes," Jonathan said. He looked back down at the table as if he was embarrassed by his own response.

"The one that was killed two days before trial?"

"Yes," Jonathan said.

"Do you feel at all personally guilty for his death?" Jenkins asked. She was completely calm, cool, and collected this time.

"I was just doing my job."

"And it seems that you're quite good at your job, aren't you?" Jenkins asked.

"I guess you could say so. I haven't been much good at anything for the past couple of years."

"But didn't you quit investigative work after the death of Mr. Walker? It had nothing to do with your wife, did it?" Jenkins asked.

"There were a lot of reasons as to why I quit. The pressure was just too much. And, yes, after the whole thing with Tyler, I began to doubt myself. I began to question my own morals. I didn't know who he was or why they wanted to locate him, I just did my job. I didn't do anything wrong, but I felt like I had," Jonathan said. A single solitary tear fell from his eye and he quickly wiped it away. Jennifer's demeanor suddenly changed and it looked like she had closed herself off. It was as if someone had turned off a switch inside her.

"What's Don Cicerone's connection to the cipher drive? How does he know about it?" Jenkins asked.

"All I know is that he hired me to get it back for him. I assumed that it was his in the first place and that it was taken from him," Jonathan said.

"But that doesn't make sense," Jenkins said. "How could he have had it first? Dr. Cobalt, what do you know about this man, Don Cicerone?" she asked.

"I don't know who he is," Jennifer said.

They had shifted their attention away from Jonathan and now directed it to Jennifer. Her faced turned bright red as if she had done something very wrong as well. She got the sinking feeling in her stomach that the two agents weren't on their side.

"You mean to tell me that you've never heard that name before?" Steiner asked.

Jennifer looked down at the table. She didn't answer the question. "Dr. Cobalt?"

"Yes?"

"Please answer the question," Jenkins said.

"I mean I've heard that name before. Sure. Who hasn't?"

"We want to know what your connection to him is."

"I don't have a connection to him," she said.

"Are you sure?" Jenkins asked. She got up and started pacing again and Jennifer's face turned bright red.

"Yes."

"I think you're lying to me, Dr. Cobalt."

"I'm not lying to you. I don't have any connection to him," Jennifer barked back. Jonathan realized that they weren't just singling him out; they were also making Jennifer feel like she had done something wrong as well. He reached over and squeezed her hand to offer some moral support.

"We have reason to believe that you do," Jenkins said. Jonathan turned and looked at Jennifer, and she looked down at the table. "We have reason to believe that he's the one that contracted you to perform the work in the first place. We have reason to believe that he's the one was behind the scenes in the Arlington, Virginia lab project. He's the private donor isn't he?"

"I don't know what you're talking about," she said.

Did Jennifer actually know Don Cicerone? Was there some connection that Jonathan had missed? He searched his memory bank. He tried to think back to something, anything that he could remember about the project. Was that why he was chosen to find her? Why would they need him? He still felt lost and confused. He didn't have any of the answers.

"Please, Dr. Cobalt. We need you to be straight with us," Jenkins said.

"Look," Jennifer said. "All I know is that I was hired by Advanced Biogenics to do the work that I'm already passionate about. I don't know about any Italian Mob Boss, or why some Russian Hit Man is out to kill me."

"I'm having a hard time believing you," Jenkins said.

"Why?" Jonathan asked. "Why wouldn't you believe her?"

"Her body language. She's hiding something," Jenkins said.

"I think you're just upsetting her. I think that's it and I think we should just move on and get this whole thing over with so that we can all go home," Jonathan said.

Jenkins gave Jonathan a stern look as if to tell him that he needed to just shut up, but she left it alone. "Fine. Dr. Cobalt, tell me about your research. I need to get more of a background on all this."

"It seems like you know everything else. Why do you even need to talk to me anymore?" Jennifer asked. Clearly, she was upset.

"Tell me about the cipher drive. Tell me about this device," Jenkins said. Steiner just sat there taking notes. The whole thing was being recorded so Jonathan wasn't sure why he was even bothering to take notes.

"It can crack anything. It can hack into any database through brute force," Jennifer said.

"And you created this knowingly? You knew what it would be used for?" Steiner asked, looking up from his notepad.

"Look, I did a job. That's all. I did what I was paid to do. I did what I loved to do," she said.

"You love breaking into things?" Jenkins asked.

"I love numbers. Ciphers get me excited. When I look at algorithms, they're sexy to me," she said. She cracked a half-smile.

"I understood that part Dr. Cobalt. Well, it seems that

the two of you have some similarities. You both are paid to do something you love, but that you know is wrong," Jenkins said. She wasn't trying to be funny at all but Jonathan laughed at that.

"What's so funny Mr. Grace?" Jenkins asked.

"Nothing," he said.

"Fine. Let's move on," Jenkins finally said.

"Let's," Jonathan said.

"God, please," Jennifer said.

"Mr. Grace. Are you prepared to do anything required of you here? Are you prepared to go the extra mile to help us bring this whole thing to a close and bring Medviek to justice?" asked Jenkins.

"Of course I am. Why wouldn't I be?"

"Well, there is the matter of your job. You've been hired to bring something back to Don Cicerone. What we need to know is that, if you're put up to this task, are you going to help us, or are you going to serve your own interests at the end of the day?"

"What does that even mean? Serve my own interests?" Jonathan asked. He knew what they were talking about, but he was surprised by the audacity of the question.

"There's some money on the line for you here isn't there?" Steiner asked.

"Yes."

"Just how much money is on the line? Just how much money will you be paid for bringing back the cipher drive? How much are they paying you for the device? It must have been enough to bring you out of so-called retirement."

"A million dollars," Jonathan said. "But things have changed now."

"How have things changed?" Jenkins asked.

Jonathan looked at Jennifer. She knew what he was talking about, but he wasn't going to come out and say it to them. He cared more about her now than he did about the cipher drive. All he wanted was for everyone to leave them alone and let them live their lives out in peace.

"They just have," Jennifer said, answering for him.

The two agents looked at her, then looked at each other. They were starting to get the picture. "So, you're willing to help us then? You're willing to help us get this device out of the hands of all of these criminals? At the very least are you willing to do that for us?" Jenkins asked.

"Yes. Of course we are," Jennifer said.

"We'll do whatever it takes," Jonathan added. "I just want this whole nightmare to be over with."

"Okay, well, we have a lot of work to do then," Jenkins said. "We should probably get started right away."

20

"Don Cicerone?" Jonathan asked, as the call connected to the voice on the other end. He hadn't spoken to the one man who he was supposed to be accountable to on the job, for days. He braced himself for what would be a difficult conversation.

"Hey kid, where the hell you been? I was about to send out a search squad. When I told you I needed constant updates, what do you do? You turn off your phone," he said.

"There have been some complications," Jonathan said, his tone melancholy.

"What kind of complications, kid?"

"The serious kind."

"You've got some explaining to do. You better start talking before I lose my cool," said the increasingly agitated voice on the other end.

"Look. There's some good news and there's some bad news," Jonathan said. "Which would you rather hear first?"

"What's the good news?" he asked.

"The good news is that I found the cipher drive," Jonathan said, trying his best to say it in the most upbeat way.

"Good job, kid. What's the bad news?"

"The bad news is that I can't get to it. I've got a bounty on my head. I'm with the doctor, but the situation has gone from bad to worse," Jonathan said.

"What do you mean you can't get it? If you know where it is, then you need to get it kid," said Don Cicerone. "I don't care what it takes. I'm not paying you to screw around here."

"It's too risky. I need your help."

"What kind of help?"

"I need bodies," Jonathan said.

"Bodies?"

"Yeah. I need goons. I've got a plan," Jonathan said.

"Goons? What? You Italian all of a sudden?" Don Cicerone chuckled on the other end of the line. Jonathan could just see the grossly overweight Don laughing to himself in New York. It sickened him.

"No. I'm serious. I can't do this without your help."

"I still don't understand what's being done," Don Cicerone said.

"I know where the cipher drive is. Have you been watching the news lately?" Jonathan asked.

"Yeah, of course, kid. Always."

"Then you know what's been going on. You know what the cipher drive is being used to do."

"Yeah. I kind of got that picture," Don Cicerone said.

"Okay, well it's important that we get it back before more damage is done," Jonathan said.

"Look. I'm not in this deal for good conscience. I don't care what someone else is doing with it. All I know is that I want back what is rightfully mine."

"Rightfully yours? It wasn't yours to begin with," Jonathan said.

"Whoa. What are you saying, kid? You forget who you're speaking to? Of course, it was rightfully mine. It belongs to me. As far as you're concerned, I'm the rightful owner. Do I need to say anything more about that?"

Jonathan could tell that the Don was getting increasingly agitated, which wasn't his intent. He tried his best to calm him down. "That's not what I meant. I'm sorry it came across that way."

"Okay kid. Apology accepted."

"Thanks. I didn't mean any disrespect. I really need your help, that's all," Jonathan said.

"Okay. I'm going to put Vinnie and Tony on a plane right now. I can have them there to you in less than 24 hours. How does that sound?" Don Cicerone asked.

"Can you spare anyone else?"

"Yeah. I'll be tagging along," he said.

"Okay. Great," Jonathan said.

"Good. Done. Istanbul it is. See you soon, kid," Don Cicerone barked into the phone just before he hung up.

"Thanks."

Jonathan looked at Jennifer as they ate at a café by the water. Agents Jenkins and Steiner were in a car not too far away, with a watchful eye on them. "What did he say?" Jennifer asked.

"It's done," Jonathan said.

"They're coming?"

"Yeah."

"That's a relief. Do you think it will work?" she asked.

"I really hope so. We're nearly out of options. I feel the pressure on all sides. I never wanted all of this. I thought this was going to be plain and simple until all these other people got involved," Jonathan said.

"I know. We'll get through it," she said. She reached over and nudged her knee against his.

"I know we will. I guess… What I mean is…"

"What?" she asked.

"When this is all over, what's going to happen next?" Jonathan asked.

"What do you mean?"

"What's going to happen with us?" Jonathan looked at her with his brown puppy-dog eyes. He looked like a wounded animal, but she adored it.

"I don't know," she said. "I guess we'll just play it by ear."

"What do you mean?" he asked.

"I was never one for planning things like that out. I think we should just let the cards fall where they may. Every time I've tried to plan on things like this, it never went well," she said.

"What's wrong with planning?" he asked.

"Nothing. That's not what I'm saying," she said.

"Oh?"

"Don't misunderstand me. I really like you. In fact, I like you a lot, probably more than I've led on to believe," she said.

Jonathan smiled after that statement. "That makes me feel better," he said.

"So, I'm not saying anything like that. I've just had a lot of… bad experiences in the past with relationships." She looked down at the table and moved the food on her plate around with her fork.

"What kind of bad experiences?" he asked. "I guess I don't really know that much about you. I feel like I've been an open book, but with you, I'm always clamoring to learn more."

"I know. It's just my personality. It's not easy for me to let people in," she said.

"Were you hurt in the past? What happened? You know what's happened with me. You know what's happened in my past," he said.

"Yeah, and it's terrible. I mean, it's more than terrible," she said. "I'm not quite sure how you managed to move on after that. I don't know how I would have handled something like that,"

"I didn't think I would ever move on either. I didn't think I could ever have any emotions or feelings for another person again. I guess you just adapt, and over time, you heal," he said.

"Do you feel heeled?" she asked. She looked at him with a puzzled look, but Jonathan melted at the site of those pale blue eyes. Her hair fell in a short cluster as she looked down at the table, almost embarrassed for asking a question like that. He just wanted to reach over and kiss her again, but he knew it wasn't the time for that.

"I don't think I can ever really be whole again, but I feel better. I feel better ever since I came here; since I met you," he said.

She smiled. "That's sweet. That's probably one of the sweetest things that anyone has ever said to me."

"Well, I really do mean it. I hope you know that," he said.

"Yeah. I do."

"But that still leaves me at not really knowing that much about you. I guess I really want to know everything about you. I don't know why. It's just something inside of me," he said.

"What else do you want to know?"

"I have so many questions."

"Like what?" she asked.

"I don't know. Like a lot of things."

"Such as what? I feel like you know mostly everything," she said, as she looked away.

"Okay, for example, when Jenkins and Steiner were questioning us, I didn't feel like you were being honest about the whole Don Cicerone thing. When they asked you if you knew him, I felt like you were lying or concealing the truth," he said.

"I do know him," she said, dropping a bomb.

"You do?"

"Yeah. I do."

"How?" he asked.

"It's a long story."

"You see, this is just one of those things… it's one of those things that I don't know about you. There are so many gaps… so many holes to fill," he said.

"I knew him through my husband," she said. She looked down at her food again and her face turned red.

"I thought you weren't married. Did you tell me that you weren't married?"

"I'm not married. I should say my late husband," she said.

"I don't get it. You see, now I'm totally lost."

"You don't need to feel lost. In fact, you're going to feel eerily close to me when I tell you this," she said.

"Tell me what?"

"I was married to Tyler Walker," she said.

"What? You're serious?"

"Yes."

"How is that possible... but... then that means that you're..." he said.

"Yes. He was the one that was going to turn state's evidence on Don Cicerone. He was the one that you helped track down for him," she said.

Jonathan's faced turned bright red. He could feel the fire heating up in his face. Now he understood why she had been so timid and resistant of him initially. It was Jonathan who was responsible for her husband's death.

"Oh my god," he said.

"Yeah. I know."

"You must hate me then?" he asked.

"Hate is a strong word," she said.

"Did you know? Did you know who I was?" he asked.

"Yes."

"And you didn't say anything?"

"I was scared to," she said.

"I didn't even put two and two together," he said.

"That's surprising. You know, I was young and stupid when we met, and I've had to pay for his mistakes. When he turned state's evidence, and after he was killed, they threatened me. They told me that I needed to do this project, or else. They were going to kill me, Jonathan. I was paid well for it, but when I realized what was being done, I wanted out; they wouldn't let me out. I was scared out of my mind."

"Which is why you came back here, isn't it?"

"Yes," she said.

"Wow," Jonathan said. He sat back in his chair and put his hand on his forehead, as if he were just about to faint. "I feel like such a jerk," he said.

"Yeah, well, you were doing your job. I guess I can't really fault you for it. You were just doing your job. You didn't know what they were going to…"

"I should have known. I shouldn't have just marched straight into that situation. He was always such a good client… Don Cicerone that is… and… well…"

"Yeah, I get it," she said.

"And now he's on his way here," he said. He clasped his hand on his mouth. "Why the hell did you agree to that? What are we going to do now?"

"Well, there's something else that I haven't really told

you," she said.

"Oh, God, what? What is it?"

"It's… You're going to hate me when I tell you this…" she said.

"No I won't," he said.

"I have a copy of the cipher," she said.

"What? The formulas?"

"No, the whole thing," she said. "The chipset with the cipher pre-loaded on USB. The whole thing."

"Holy shit."

"Yeah."

"There's two of them out there?" he asked.

"Yes."

"Do they know that?"

"No. I created a duplicate for myself. I kept it for protection. In case anything ever was to happen to me or my family, I had to keep it for insurance purposes. No one else is supposed to have that. The power that it holds is tremendous. You don't understand, Jonathan; you can do anything with that cipher. You can hack into anything as long as you know what you're doing."

"Okay, all of this is starting to make a lot more sense to me," he said.

"Are you going to say anything? Are you going to tell

them what I just told you?"

"No, of course not."

"Thank you," she said.

"But what the hell are we going to do now? We had this whole thing planned out. Why didn't you say something sooner? Why didn't you just tell me all of it before?" he asked.

"I didn't think I could trust you. I really didn't. I thought you were here to kill me at first, but then when you saved me like that… I don't know… It all just has happened so fast. It's hard for me to trust people. I hope you can understand how much I've been through. This has taken such an enormous toll on me. I feel like I've aged twenty years in a matter of two," she said.

If she had aged twenty years in a matter of two then Jonathan certainly didn't notice it. She was still the most beautiful woman he had ever met, by far. "I guess I should feel good about that."

"It's just been hard on me… it's been hard for me to trust people. Everyone that I've put my trust in has burned me… everyone other than my immediate family. Does that make sense to you? I've been on edge for so long. It's been so frustrating. I couldn't even begin to sit here and explain it to you," she said.

"I understand. It makes sense. I guess I just... I don't know what I..." Jonathan was fumbling for his words. He was searching for the right thing to say, but he didn't know what to say at all. "You can trust me. I'm not going to burn you," he finally said.

"I don't feel like you would. But, then again, I didn't feel like I would get burned any other time. I've been paying for someone else's mistakes for years now. Do you see how they've had me in this noose for so long?" she asked.

"Yes. I can see. What I don't understand is how Jenkins and Steiner didn't make the connection between you and Tyler. Did you change your last name?" he asked.

"I never assumed his last name."

"Still... I don't see how they wouldn't have made the connection."

"I don't know either. I guess they just didn't say anything or they don't know," she added.

"They seem to be in the know about everything else. Maybe that was why they said you were lying to them. Maybe they knew and they're just trying to hold onto their cards. Maybe they know even more than they're letting on to know. Who knows with them," he said. "They certainly acted weird in there, didn't they?"

"Yes. I didn't feel like they were on our side at all."

"Neither did I," he said.

"So, what do we do now?" she asked.

"Now, we just go along with their plan," he replied.

"What if Don Cicerone… what if… what if he asks you to…"

"I'm not going to let anything bad happen to you," he said. "Plus, we have insurance now. We have another cipher drive. We need to put our heads together. We need to come up with our own game plan."

"What did you have in mind?"

"Okay. Here's what we're going to do…"

They spoke about the details of their plan. They sat there strategizing, thinking of all the other options. They thought about all the different contingencies that they could come up with. Jonathan realized that she was much smarter than she had led on. He realized that there was so much more to her than meets the eye. And, there was a lot too look at when it came to her appearance, that was for certain. But, there was also a depth to her that he hadn't found in anyone else. Maybe he was attracted to the desperation in her. Maybe he just wanted to help her heal her past wounds. Whatever it was, it was strong. He felt compelled, in fact, to help her. He was drawn to her like steel to a magnet. It was undeniably strong.

21

Don Cicerone and his goons stepped off the private jet in Istanbul, Turkey, just 16 hours after having gotten off the phone with Jonathan. They quickly cleared immigration, paid for their visiting visas, and entered the country. The three Italians were completely out of their element. Gone was the New York City backdrop that they were so accustomed to, only to be replaced with the uncertainty of a foreign environment. Their gaudy thick gold chains and black tee shirts were stereotypically tacky. But they were none the wiser and they couldn't have cared less. They were there for one purpose and one purpose only – for the cipher. After years of investing his time and money into the lab for development of the cipher, Don Cicerone was anxious to get it back into his hands.

He was anxious to possess the power of the small device. He couldn't think of anything more. It kept him up at night thinking about various ways he would use it for his own personal gain. But he knew he couldn't do it on his own. He knew that the cipher drive needed more than just a willing person to insert it into a computer – it needed a skilled technician. His motivations were for more than just the cipher drive; he was also after Dr. Cobalt. She was the one that knew how to use the cipher drive and implement it in ways that seldom few could dream of. But, without the cipher drive, he had nothing. His first goal was secure the cipher drive, but the second was for Dr. Cobalt. If he couldn't get Dr. Cobalt, then no one would.

He walked through the airport terminal with his goons, Vinnie and Tony, as they made their way towards the airport exit and into the awaiting luxury sedan. He thought about Jonathan and the doctor as the car pulled away from the airport. It was all he could think of as they were quickly whisked off towards a hotel in Taksim Square, a central square in Istanbul. Don Cicerone picked up his phone and quickly punched in the last number that Jonathan had called him from.

"Kid?"

"Don Cicerone? Are you in already?" Jonathan asked.

"Yeah, we're here."

"Great. We only have a few hours," Jonathan said.

"A few hours for what kid?"

"A few hours until the exchange."

"Stop speaking in riddles, kid. What do you mean?" asked the Don, clearly agitated by the direction the conversation was taking.

"I'll explain when you get settled in," Jonathan said.

"Meet us at the hotel. Taksim Square in one hour," barked the Italian mob boss into the cellphone.

"Okay. Will do."

"Oh, and kid?"

"Yeah?"

"You better not screw this up. I can't tell you how important that cipher drive is to me. I need to have it back in my hands, no matter what the cost. Don't even think you'll do anything but help me out here. Remember, I gave you this opportunity. No one else did. No matter what you've heard about the cipher drive from anyone, it still belongs to me. Don't be getting any screwy ideas, do you hear me?"

"Yes, of course," Jonathan said.

"Where's the girl? Where's Dr. Cobalt?"

"Here, with me," Jonathan said. He gave an uneasy look at Jennifer.

"Perfect. Don't lose sight of her. Make sure she comes with you."

"Okay," Jonathan said, clicking the phone shut.

He looked at Jennifer after the conversation. He realized that there was more of a motivation to locate her than he had originally suspected, but he didn't want to spook her. He didn't feel the need to upset her more than she already was at the time. He could see it in her eyes. He could tell just how nervous and afraid she was. He wanted to protect her and comfort her. He wanted to be everything he could be to her, but he knew there was only so much that he could do. The cards were going to fall where they would. Soon, only time would tell just how things would work out. He hoped and prayed that they would work out in their favor.

"What did he say?" Jennifer asked.

"He said to meet him in Taksim Square in an hour. They're checking into the hotel soon and we need to be ready to go," Jonathan said.

"Have you talked to Agent Jenkins? Are they all set and ready to go?" she asked.

"Yes. I just sent her a text. Everything is all set," he said.

"Jonathan?" she said, leaning forward to grab his hand.

"Yeah?"

"I'm scared."

"I know. Me too. It's going to be okay. We're going to get through this, I promise you. I won't let anything bad happen to you," he said.

"How did we get ourselves wrapped up in this situation? How did we find ourselves in this dilemma?" she asked.

"I don't know, but we're in it and we'll deal with it. There's nothing else we can do. There's no sense in worrying yourself sick now about all of it."

"I know," she said, "but I can't help it. It's just in my nature."

"What are you so worried about? He's here for the cipher drive. He's not going to hurt you," Jonathan said, but he wasn't entirely sure if that was true.

"I wouldn't be so sure of that," she said.

"Why would you say that?" Jonathan asked.

"I don't know. Maybe it's because I'm the one who created it, and I'm one of the few people in the world that can harness its true potential."

"You mean, the way in which Medviek is doing?" Jonathan said in an attempt to break the ice, but the joke went over her head.

"That's not even funny."

"Sorry."

Jennifer crossed her arms in front of her in the chair. "That was a stupid thing to say. You don't realize what this cipher drive is do you?"

"I mean I get it," Jonathan said.

"Do you really though? Do you really understand the potential of it? This is weapons-grade cryptography. With the cipher drive, I could virtually login onto a nuclear missile silo and bypass the security code, keys, and verbal authentications, and singlehandedly launch a missile. I could do that from anywhere in the world," she said.

An ominous look replaced Jonathan's earlier smile. "Seriously?"

"Yes, seriously."

"Whoa. That's heavy."

"Yes, I know," she said.

"I can see why he wants it back so badly."

"You don't even know the half of it." She unfolded her arms and looked off to the side towards the ocean. Jonathan admired her profile. He admired her long slender neck, her raised cheekbones, and her silky blonde hair. He admired all of her.

"It sounds bad. Now I see why he was willing to pay a million dollars to get it back."

"I'm surprised he only offered you only a million. It's worth billions, maybe more, and I'm not even exaggerating. You could break into any bank anywhere in the world and siphon off any amount of money. I don't think Medviek really understands what he has," she said.

"No, I think that he does. I just think that he hasn't used it to its full potential yet. But, aside from bringing the whole world into a complete state of chaos and destruction, he's probably been using it very efficiently," Jonathan said.

"Well, it sounds like it."

Agent Jenkins and Steiner appeared as they walked up to meet with the pair who had been waiting for them to arrive.

"Hey guys," they said in unison.

"Hi," Jonathan said.

"Hey," Jennifer said, looking down at her feet.

"Are they here? Are they in town?" Jenkins asked.

"Yes," Jonathan said. "Now what?"

"Now it's go time," Steiner said.

*****

Boris Medviek stood at the stern of his superyacht with

his brother Dmitry. They watched as the ocean disappeared behind them as they steamed just off the coast of Istanbul.

"How many hours before Sheik Abdullah gets here?" asked Dmitry.

"Six."

"Are we all set with the list?"

"Yes."

"What if something goes wrong?"

"Like what?" Boris asked.

"I don't know. What if?"

"We deal with it. What could go wrong? We have the list and we have the cipher drive," Boris said.

"But we don't have the girl. The doctor is still here somewhere," Dmitry said.

"Now whose fault is that?"

"Viktor's of course."

"And who decided to bring Viktor in on this?" Boris asked.

"I did," Dmitry said. He looked off towards the sunset as they stood at their customary positions at the railing by the stern.

"You see that bird," Boris said, pointing to the white seagull that was tracking the yacht closely. .

"Yeah."

"What do you think that bird is doing following this yacht so closely?"

"I don't know. Looking for food maybe?"

"That seagull is an opportunist," Boris said. "It's not just looking for us to throw it food. That seagull, like the other seagulls nearby, is waiting for an opportunity. Whether it's for the fish that come up to the water when the yacht passes over the ocean, or it's waiting for something to fall off this yacht, it's hovering close by, waiting for that opportunity."

"Okay. What's your point?" Dmitry asked.

"You see. Unlike his fellow seagulls that are flying off to the side and further behind, this seagull is flying almost right behind us. It's almost predatory. It's more than an opportunist. It's waiting for the perfect moment until it can strike. Unlike Viktor, this seagull will succeed in its life."

"So what you're saying is that we need more seagulls like you?" Dmitry asked, laughing.

Boris shook his head. "You don't understand little brother. That's okay. I don't expect you to understand everything. What I expect you to do is deliver results. When you told me that the girl wouldn't be a problem, I trusted you. I left it in your hands because I thought that you would be capable of taking care of this. This is the entire reason why we came here in the first place."

"I understand brother. Again, I'm sorry."

"If you weren't my brother, you would have been swimming in the ocean with the fish by now," Boris said. "Even if you are only my half-brother, you are still blood."

"I know. Thank you. I'll make it up to you."

"I know you will," Boris said.

Dmitry looked off into the distance as his cell phone rang. Boris looked at him, and Dmitry stared at the phone. "Speak of the devil," Dmitry said. "It's Viktor."

"Well. What are you waiting for? Answer it."

Dmitry picked up the phone. "Da?" He looked at Boris. "He wants to speak to you."

Boris snatched the phone away from his brother. "What?" he barked into the phone.

"I'm following them now. They're in a taxi getting out at Taksim Square. What do you want me to do?" asked Viktor.

"Keep following them. Don't lose them," Boris yelled into the phone.

"Okay." He clicked the phone shut and handed it back to his brother.

"What now?"

"They're on foot. They're in Taksim Square," Boris said.

"What should we do?" Dmitry asked.

"Send the message," Boris said, holding onto the handrails and watching as the blue ocean disappeared into the background, and watched as the city of Istanbul came back into the horizon as they neared the docks again.

"You sure?" Dmitry asked.

"I'm sure."

22

Jonathan and Jennifer entered the hotel and sat down in the lobby. They didn't notice Viktor nearby in the car, watching them, but the agents tipped them off as to his presence. He had parked just outside the lobby and tipped the valet to keep a close watch on them. He thought he was being inconspicuous; he thought he was hidden and out of site, ready to strike at a moment's notice. He smiled to himself as he watched and waited for them to reemerge.

"What do we do now?" Jennifer asked.

"Now we wait. They should be down any moment."

"Then what?"

"Then we stick to the plan," Jonathan said.

"Okay." She reached over, grabbed his hand, and squeezed it again. He could sense the nervousness in her weak grip. He could feel her cold, sweaty hands as they trembled in anticipation of what was to come.

"It's going to be okay. I promise." He looked at her with nervous unease.

"I know. I trust you."

"Do you have it with you?" he asked.

"Yes. It's in my pocket," she said. Pointing to the small bulge in her blue jeans.

"Is that really it?"

"Yeah."

"Let me see it," he said.

She whipped it out of her pocket and handed it to him. It was an exact duplicate of the black USB cipher drive. Jonathan cupped it in his hands and looked down at it. It was such a small and almost harmless looking device. "You mean this is what it looks like. This is what they're after?"

"Yes," she said.

"But it looks so… so…"

"Harmless?" she asked.

"Yeah."

"I know, but it's not. You know what this is. You know

exactly what this is."

"How did you do it? Weren't you afraid that they would find out?"

"Of course. But, like I said before, it's for security. And there's another one in a safety deposit box. This one isn't the real thing. This one is just the chipset without the cipher ingrained on it."

"What do you mean?" Jonathan asked.

"It doesn't have my algorithms on it. This is just the shell, but we're not going to tell them that," she said.

"Do you want me to hang onto it?" Jonathan asked.

"Yes. You hold it. You keep it," she said. She slipped the slim USB drive into his front pocket, leaned forward, and gave him a quick kiss on the lips, just as Don Cicerone and his goons reached the lobby.

"Look what we have here," he said, as he walked up with his mini- entourage. Jonathan remembered Vinnie from New York, but it was his first encounter with Tony. He was shocked to find that he was even more overweight than the Don himself.

"Hi," Jonathan said, quickly standing up. Jennifer joined him.

"Hey," she said sheepishly.

"It's good to see you here doc," said the Don.

Jennifer looked at the ground and didn't respond. Jonathan was still busy observing Tony's triple chin that seemed to be stained with some sort of white sauce. He pointed to Tony. "You've got some stuff… here… on your chin," Jonathan said. He wasn't sure why that was important at the time, but he wasn't sure how else to break the awkwardness of the moment.

"Where? Here?" Tony asked, as he tried to wipe away what was there.

"Yeah. It's gone," Jonathan said.

Don Cicerone looked on with incredulity. "Hey… you… who cares?" he asked.

"Sorry," Jonathan said.

"Now. About the cipher drive," Don Cicerone said.

"Medviek has it," Jonathan said.

"Who?"

"Boris Medviek. The Russian who's been causing all of the chaos in the news. I told you I would explain it to you in person, and there it is," Jonathan added.

"Where is he, kid? Where is this Medviek character?"

"On a yacht. Here in port. The other side of the bridge, but we need a plan," Jonathan said.

"The plan is, we go in there and start blasting," Vinnie said.

"It's not going to be as simple as that. This guy is sophisticated. He has money, guns, and the bodies to take us all out," Jonathan said.

"We'll see about that," Don Cicerone said. "What do you think, doc? What's your take on all of this?"

"I just want my life back," she said. She looked down at the ground. It was the one man who had made her life miserable for years. She had sworn she would never see him again, and there she was standing right in front of him in her own country. She was disgusted by it all but knew there wasn't a thing she could do. She had put her trust in Jonathan, the agents, and the plan. If it all went south, she was dead, and Jonathan would probably be, as well.

"You'll get it back. That is the last thing I need from you," Don Cicerone said.

"Here's the plan," Jonathan said. "There's a car outside this hotel. Inside of it, is a man named Viktor. He's tried to kill us twice before. He works for Medviek. We need Viktor to get access to Medviek."

"So we go out there and start blasting?" Vinnie said again. Jonathan looked at him with disgust. He had brought along a man with a single-track mind. There was no arguing with him; he was going to start blasting at the first opportunity he could get.

"And cause an international incident in the middle of one of the busiest squares in the city? No. That's not how we go about this," Jonathan said.

"So, what's your bright idea, kid?" Don Cicerone asked.

"We need to work together on this. Look, Medviek knows that you're the one who commissioned the work at Advanced Biogenics; right?" Jonathan asked.

"No, I don't know that. How would he know that?" Don Cicerone asked.

"Well, he's the one who broke in and stole the thing from there. He must have gotten wind it was in development. How else did he know when to go and where to strike?" Jonathan asked.

"That's something I don't know yet. I'm still working on that," Don Cicerone said. He gave Jennifer a long stern look, as if to tell her she was far from out of the woods just yet.

"Well, that's my take on it," Jonathan said.

"If we need to use Viktor out there to get to Medviek," Vinnie said, "then, how do we do that? Do you think Medviek cares if one of his hired hit men lives or dies?"

"No, but he will care if he thinks that we have a copy of the cipher drive," Jonathan said.

Jennifer gave him a long look, as if she were about to

slap him in the face. He could read her mind, but it was part of his plan; it was the only way to get out of it scot-free.

"What do you mean?" Don Cicerone asked.

"What if I told you that we have a copy of the cipher drive?" Jonathan said.

"I wouldn't believe you," Don Cicerone said.

"Well, let's just say for all intensive purposes, that we do have a copy."

"Prove it," said the thick-necked Italian mob boss.

Jonathan slipped his fingers into his pocket and produced the tiny device from his pocket.

"Voilà!" Jonathan exclaimed.

The three Italians stood there staring at him. Don Cicerone looked at Jonathan in the eyes as if he was going to reach over and strangle him, take the cipher drive, and bolt.

"Where the hell did you get that kid?" Don Cicerone and his goons started to walk towards him when Jonathan lifted up his shirt briefly to expose the gun hidden in his waist.

"Not so fast," Jonathan cooed quietly. "Do you want to make a scene here?" Jonathan added.

"Look at this. Kid's got some balls, don't he?" said Tony. "Let's blast him right here!"

"No. Not like this," Don Cicerone said as he reached out two pudgy hands to stop them dead in their tracks. "Explain kid, and fast."

"Okay. Here's what we do. We get out there and tell Viktor we have the cipher drive, and that we're also armed. We make him take us to Boris. Then, we improvise," Jonathan, said. He looked at Jennifer as if to try to make her feel more at ease, but she was shifting her weight from one leg to the other as if she was preparing to run for her life.

"Improvise?" asked Vinnie.

"Yeah. Improvise. You know, make stuff up as we go?" Jonathan said with a sly grin on his face.

"This isn't a game kid. If you had that cipher drive the whole time, then you're going to get a cap in that skull of yours as soon as you're not paying attention," Don Cicerone said.

"No, I haven't had it the entire time."

Don Cicerone looked over at Jennifer. "You made more than one? Why you sly little…"

"Hey," Jonathan barked, "No need for any of that!"

"It's okay, Jonathan," Jennifer said.

"No, it's not okay," he yelled, catching the attention of people walking through the expansive hotel lobby.

"Look. We do as the kid says," Don Cicerone said.

"We're going to listen to this little putz?" Tony asked.

"Yeah. We are. For now. We need to get that other cipher drive, and I want this Medviek's head on a platter, so let's march," Don Cicerone said. "Let's go, kid. Lead the way," he added.

Jonathan led them all outside, keeping a close eye on the Italians and the Russian Hit Man in the car. Viktor saw them coming and pretended not to pay attention. It was laughable to Jonathan. They walked up to the car and knocked on the window. Viktor looked like a deer in headlights. He rolled down the window as Don Cicerone stood there with his two goons by his side while Jonathan and Jennifer stood off to the side. As Don Cicerone stood at the passenger window, the two goons got into the backseat of the car, pulled out their guns, and pointed them at Viktor.

"I think we have ourselves a little problem," Don Cicerone said to Viktor.

"Problem?" asked Viktor. His eyes darted to the rearview mirror and then to the backseat where the two thick-necked triple-chinned Italians sat with their hands on their triggers.

"Not so fast," Don Cicerone said as Viktor tried to reach for his gun. He opened his suit jacket to reveal his own gun. "I think three to one you might have a problem."

"What do you want?" Viktor asked. "I don't want any trouble."

"You've already got trouble," Don Cicerone said. "Now, it just depends on how much more trouble you're going to get." He smiled after he said it and Viktor could see his the three gold crowns in his front teeth. He knew he was in trouble.

"Please. I'm just doing my job," Viktor said.

Don Cicerone motioned for Jonathan and Jennifer to get in the car as he climbed in the passenger seat. "It's going to be a tight squeeze," Don Cicerone said as Jennifer climbed onto Jonathan's lap in order to cram into the back of the dark sedan.

Don Cicerone whipped out his gun and pointed it at Viktor. "Now drive," he said, gritting his teeth as he said it. "Take me to Medviek now."

Viktor was bumbling his words. It was the first time Jonathan and Jennifer had seen him like that. The once stone-cold killer was now shivering in his pants. Jonathan had to smile to himself for a moment at that thought. He had to revel in the power that the small group now held.

"I... I... I can't," Viktor said.

There were now four guns pointed at the Russian Hit

Man. Jonathan pulled his out, as well. They all stared at him, waiting for the next move.

"Pick up the phone and call him now. We have something that he wants," Don Cicerone said.

"You do?" Viktor asked, as if there were a bright light to the whole situation.

"Tell him we have the cipher drive. The only other cipher drive in existence," Jonathan said.

Viktor picked up the phone and dialed Dmitry's number as all four guns moved closer to Viktor's chest and back, as if to tell him he had better watch his mouth on the phone.

"Put Boris on the phone," Viktor said. There was silence for a moment.

"Da?' Boris said from the other end. The entire car could hear the conversation on speakerphone.

"I have some… some news," Viktor said.

"What is it?"

"I have the doctor… and I have the cipher drive…"

"What do you mean you have the cipher drive?" Boris said.

"I have the second cipher drive and the doctor. She wants to speak to you in person," Viktor said. He was tumbling his words but doing a good enough job on the phone not to spook Boris.

"There's another cipher drive? That's not possible."

"Yes," Viktor said.

"Come to the yacht right away. We're at the dock. Hurry up because I have an important appointment arriving in one hour," Boris said. He was referring to the Sheik's arrival via helicopter.

"Okay. I'm on my way," Viktor said.

"Viktor?" Boris barked into the phone.

"Da?"

"What about the friend? The detective? Jonathan Grace? Where is he?" Viktor went silent for a moment as Don Cicerone jabbed the phone into his stomach.

"I have them... both of them..."

"Perfect. You're not that useless after all, are you?"

"I'm leaving now. I'll be there in 30 minutes," Viktor said.

"Goodbye." Boris clicked the phone shut.

23

The black EC155 helicopter held low to the ground as its thunderous propellers resonated over the sea on its distant approach to Boris Medviek's white superyacht, glistening in the high summer sun. The chopper had been fitted with the latest stealth technology, making it completely transparent to radar. Coupled with the low flying altitude, it went entirely unnoticed by all Air Traffic Control Systems. Sheik Abdullah leaned in as the EC155 approached over windless skies to get a better look at the yacht as it sat anchored at the port of Istanbul. He picked up his phone and dialed

Medviek.

"We're on final approach," said the Sheik as Medviek answered the line. The chopper circled around twice to ensure that the area was clear of any authorities. The sensitivity of the material being transferred would have national governments on high alert across the entire globe. The Sheik knew the importance of the transaction, and he knew he could never be too careful. He knew all too well that things could go very wrong.

"I can see that you've circled a couple of times. Nervous, are we?" Boris asked.

"One can never be too cautious," replied the Sheik.

"That's very true."

"And the list?"

"Right here," said Boris.

"Perfect. I will speak to you momentarily," said the Sheik. And with that, he clicked off his phone, and held onto the window railing as the chopper began its final descent onto the massive vessel's helicopter landing pad. Boris walked towards the pad with several of the yacht's deckhands and Dmitry. As the chopper wound down its engines, the propeller came to a stop and Sheik Abdullah disembarked onto the yacht along with his security personnel. The ex-military hired guns were neatly clad in black suits and dark sunglasses. Boris walked up to shake the Sheik's hand as the propellers came to a stop.

"Very good to see you," Boris said.

"It's very good to be here," said the Sheik. "I have waited patiently for this day for quite some time now," he added.

"Yes, I know."

They walked towards the upper deck seating area and took their spots at the table, which had been prearranged for the Sheik's arrival. Plates of cheeses, fine wines, and an assortment of other food and drink adorned the luxuriously-appointed outdoor dining area.

"Please sit," Boris said, motioning the Sheik to the table. Boris sat opposite him, and the others took their seats at the table. Dmitry sat between the Sheik and Boris.

"Thank you. Once again, you've proved to be a very gracious host," said the Sheik.

"It's all my pleasure. I am thrilled to have you back here," Boris said.

"What, no women this time?" asked the Sheik, smiling.

"Of course. But I thought we would handle our business first, then get to the pleasure part."

"That sounds like a good plan."

"So, tell me, did you face much difficulty obtaining that

list?" asked the Sheik.

"You know how heavily guarded that list is," Dmitry said.

"Yes, of course," replied the Sheik.

"Then you can only imagine the lengths that we've gone to in order to secure those names," Boris said as a glass of sparking water was poured for him.

"Can I offer you any white wine, Your Highness?" asked a deckhand as he made his way around the table to the Sheik.

"Normally I wouldn't drink an ounce of alcohol. But this calls for a bit of a celebration and I'm willing to bend the rules just a little bit. Red wine please. I'm not a fan of white wine," said the Sheik, smiling from ear-to-ear.

"Right away," said the deckhand.

"You do realize that we'll have to verify the list at random," said the Sheik as he took a sip of his red wine. "Excellent wine," he added.

"I'm glad you approve," Boris said.

"Of course, you may verify any of the names on the list," Dmitry said.

"We will have to choose two dozen at random for verification," said the Sheik.

"No problem," Boris said. "I would tell you that you

could verify the entire list, but it wouldn't be prudent of me to allow you to do that before the transaction is completed."

"Of course. I understand. Two-dozen names will be suitable. How many names have we on the list."

"All of them," Boris said.

"All of them?" the Sheik asked.

"Yes. *All of them.*"

The Sheik coughed as he swallowed down the wine, as if he actually couldn't believe what was being said. "I didn't think you were serious about that before," he added.

"I'm always serious when it comes to business," Boris said.

"I can see that now. Well, I must raise a glass to you for pulling off the seemingly unimaginable. This list will buy me the power and influence that I need amongst my Arab neighbors. We will no longer have to hide in the shadows while the oppressors overreach and track our every step we take. We can now do the tracking and evading," said the Sheik.

"Wonderful. I hope that the list will bring you everything that you may hope that it will," Boris said.

"Yes, it most certainly will."

"Shall we get to it then?" Boris asked.

The Sheik looked around, as if he was awaiting some military coup to occur as teams swarmed in from everywhere as the transaction went down. But, there was nothing but the sound of the lapping waves at the base of the ship and the seagulls' cries in the air.

"Yes, please," said the Sheik.

Boris disappeared for a brief moment, then reappeared with his laptop. The Sheik ordered a man in his entourage to prepare with his own laptop for the verification process. Both men opened their laptops, which whirred to life, and space was made on the very crowded table for the two very sophisticated pieces of machinery.

"Okay, here we are. All set," said Ali, the Sheik's head of security, as he prepared to vet the names on the list.

"I hope that you're prepared with a secure and very encrypted connection," said Boris.

"Of course," said Ali. "Shall we begin?"

"Yes. Let's get started," Boris replied. "The first name on the list, Mark Steven Abrahams, CIA, black-ops. Location: Riyadh."

"Confirming: Mark Steven Abrahams. Hold on please," Ali said, as his fingers glided across the keyboard in a swift motion. The beads of sweat could be seen collecting on the side of his head and along the slender black frames of his opticals. The partially-balding man looked as anxious as one person could be, but he was attempting to keep his cool. You could see the utter fear and anxiety written all over his face as he glanced around, his fingers continuing to quickly glide over the keyboard. He pushed up his glasses as they slid down his nose. "Still confirming..." he said again as he continued the process. "Okay, confirmed."

"Excellent," said the Sheik. "Next name?"

Boris looked through the list, picked more names at random, and read them off. As each name was read, a moment of silence was heard before the name was confirmed. They continued through the list of names until two-dozen had been confirmed.

"So of the 3,486 names on the list, two dozen at pure random have been confirmed," said the Sheik.

"Excellent," Boris replied. "Now, shall we discuss the transfer of the funds?"

"Of course. We are prepared to send the wire," Ali said, and the Sheik nodded his head in accordance with that statement.

"I must say," said the Sheik, "I'm still in a state of shock that you were able to pull this off. I'm not sure if you understand what this means."

"I do," said Boris nonchalantly.

"Well, if you understand, you are certainly very humble about it," replied the Sheik.

"We understand the sensitivity of this just as much as you do," said Dmitry as he scarfed down a piece of cheese with a cracker.

"I'm glad that you are all very modest about it. I want to thank you again for all of this," said the Sheik.

"No, it's us who should thank you," Boris said, and they all smiled at one another and nodded in agreement. And, Boris smiled even further as he began to read off the numbered accounts that he wanted the funds transferred to in exchange for the list.

"So, can we verify the amount being transferred?" Dmitry asked with a smile on his face.

"I see that someone is excited about this transaction," said the Sheik as he looked at the eager-eyed Dmitry.

"Yes, I cannot hide it," Dmitry said.

"That's okay. I still recall one of my first really big deals in business. I would equate it to something like that."

"Well, it's not to say that we have not done any very big deals similar to this," said Dmitry.

"I understand. That's not what I meant," said the Sheik.

"Of course. We understand what you meant. This is in fact a big deal for us," Boris said. "Please, pay no attention to my brother. He can let his ego get in the way at times." He looked over at his brother with scathing eyes. He glared at him for only a brief moment, but long enough to let him know that he needed to watch his tongue.

"So, Sheik, if I can ask you what you'll do with the names once our deal here is complete?" asked Dmitry. It was another stupid question, which only further irritated Boris.

"Please… Please… you don't have to answer that question," Boris said.

"No, no. That's quite all right. Your brother is curious. That's okay. This list is ten times more valuable to me than it is to you."

"Why is that?" Dmitry asked.

"Well, on the black market, I can sell each name for $10 million US dollars," said the Sheik. "Although it would take a tremendous amount of time for me to do that, it's not my intention."

"Oh?" asked Dmitry.

"My intention is… well… shall we say, much more sinister than that."

"How so?" asked Dmitry.

"Well, my family was brutally murdered at the hands of agents like this – agents that hid in the shadows in an attempt to conceal their true identities. These agents had no regard for my family or for me. That was many years ago but I haven't forgotten any of it. I vowed to have my revenge one day, and this is part of the plan. I've amassed a fortune greater than most others on this earth, and one of my intentions is to enact my revenge. You will undoubtedly not hear about a single thing that happens to any of these agents in the news. Why is that? Because they are all but ghosts. Their respective governments will cease to admit that they exist, let alone work for them."

Dmitry sat back after he had heard the Sheik speak, and gulped down hard. He hadn't realized the type of person that they had been dealing with. He was ruthless, cold, and calculated. He had seemed so mild- mannered, when in fact, he was exactly the opposite. And, as the Sheik was speaking, Ali's fingers continued gliding along his laptop's keyboard and so did Boris's. It was like watching two masters at work as they keyed in data and watched the output returned.

"Are we almost ready?" asked Boris.

"Yes. Almost," replied Ali.

"I do have one request to ask of you." The Sheik broke the silence of rapidly clicking keys.

"Sure, name it," Dmitry said, as his brother was still busy transferring data from the list into one composite file.

"The cipher drive," said the Sheik.

Boris's fingers stopped moving for a moment as he looked at the Sheik to witness his expression of amusement. "What about the cipher drive?" Boris asked.

"I would like to see it."

"Who told you about the cipher drive?" asked Dmitry.

"Come now. You think after all of this that I don't have the resources to find out how you've gotten your hands on this information?" The Sheik smiled at the group as he said the words.

"Well, that's not part of our deal," Boris replied, his fingers suspended in mid-air.

"Please. Wouldn't you entertain an old friend? I want to see what the source of all of this beautiful information is. I want to see the device that helped track down this data. I've only seen it in my dreams," said the Sheik.

Boris smiled. "You want to see the cipher drive?"

"Yes."

"Here it is," Boris said. He pulled out the black USB cipher drive from his pocket and held it up in the sunlight between his thumb and index finger. " A thing of beauty isn't it?" he asked.

The Sheik sat there staring at the cipher drive in absolute amazement. It wasn't that the drive looked beautiful, as the non-descript black sliver was nothing to marvel at aside from what it contained within. "Beautiful. Absolutely beautiful," said the Sheik.

Boris slipped the cipher drive back into his pocket and continued punching away at the keys as he wrapped up the compilation of the list. "I'm almost done," he said.

"Us too," Ali said.

After they had both completed their whirlwind of typing, they spun the computers towards each other and reviewed one another's work. They carefully studied the screens of each other's laptops to ensure that everything was in order. When they were all satisfied, the Sheik spoke up. "There we have it. Shall we initiate the transfer?" he asked.

"Yes, let's get this wrapped up," Dmitry replied.

"Da," said Boris, as he flashed one of his very rare expressions: a smile.

24

Agents Jenkins and Steiner tailed Viktor's car, making sure that they stayed far enough behind not to be spotted. They watched as it wound through the streets of Istanbul, crossing over the Bosporus Bridge and onto the other side. Jenkins was at the wheel and watched the vehicle carefully for any sudden movements.

"What do you think they're saying right now?" Steiner asked.

"Who knows?" said Jenkins. "The six of them are crammed in there like a can of sardines."

"Yeah, it's pretty funny looking from here."

"I know," Jenkins said, as she did her best to crack a smile and not take the situation so seriously.

"What are we going to do if that list gets out?" Steiner asked.

"I don't know. We're all going to be in a world of hurt, though, if it does. NSA Director Edwards already briefed the President on the potential that it may happen," Jenkins replied.

"This is going to be catastrophic if it does. Our jobs will be on the line."

"Our jobs? Think about all those unsuspecting agents around the world whose lives are going to be on the line. This is more than just about jobs, Geoff, it is about lives. There are people's lives at stake, and their families' lives." Jenkins frowned at Steiner as she spoke.

"I know… It's our lives at stake, too… I didn't mean to sound brash or inconsiderate… that's not what I meant… I mean… what I'm try to say is… sorry."

"Oh, it's okay. I know what you meant. But, it's not always about you. It's about other people too. Don't sound so selfish," she said, jabbing him in the stomach. She tried to make light of the situation. The more time they spent together, the more they sounded like a married couple.

"Okay, thanks," he said, smiling back at her. He kept a careful eye on the car they were tailing the entire time. The reputed Russian Hit Man had been on the US's radar for some time now, but there wasn't much they could do to arrest him there. They had to let things play out.

"I'm going to give Director Edwards a status update," Steiner said, realizing that they were getting closer to the dock.

"Okay, call him," Jenkins said.

Steiner picked up the phone, jabbed at the screen a few times quickly with his fingers, and placed the phone to his ear. Jenkins could hear Director Edwards even though the phone wasn't on speakerphone.

"Sir?" asked Steiner.

"Yes, I'm here. What's the update?" Director Edwards asked.

"We're en route to the yacht," Steiner said.

"Okay. Let me know when you arrive there."

"Will do, sir. Oh, and what about the Turkish authorities? We'll need some coordination with them in order to carry out the arrests."

"I have direct approval from the President on this and we have the full cooperation of the Turkish authorities. They're at your disposal when you need them," Director

Edwards said.

"Thank you, sir," Steiner said, and he hung up the phone.

"Okay, so we're set for the docks then?" Jenkins asked.

"Yes, all set. I'm sending a message now to the tactical team on site there. They have eyes on the yacht. SWAT is going to take their positions and will be standing by. Snipers will be on the roofs in the surrounding buildings by the dock. Hopefully those two remember to insert and turn on their hidden earpieces when they get to the docks. This is going to be a very delicate mission. Too many variables can go wrong here," Steiner said.

"Tell me about it," she replied.

*****

Jonathan and Jennifer were still stuck in the back of Viktor's sedan with the two Italian goons. Viktor was taking them to the yacht and it was either going to lead to their demise or their victory – they both knew that. They knew that things could go horribly wrong and their plan could go south.

"Are we there yet?" asked Vinnie, chuckling to himself.

"Wise guy, huh?" asked Tony, then he laughed to himself as well. Jennifer looked at Jonathan and they both rolled their eyes. They were close to the docks, and they both knew that. They knew that the teams would be prepared when they arrived, but they didn't know how things were going to go down. They were going to have to improvise.

When the car came to a halt at the parking lot, the group got out and started the walk to the yacht. Viktor, who was walking next to Don Cicerone, grabbed his hand as the phone went to his ear.

"Hey," the Don said.

"I'm just calling the boss. I'm calling Boris," Viktor said.

"Keep it on speakerphone," Vinnie said as he jabbed his gun into Viktor's back. "And no Russian!"

Viktor swallowed hard as he felt the gun in the small of his back. The group could hear the phone ringing as they made their way towards the dock. "Okay," he said.

Dmitry answered the phone. "Da?"

"I'm here," Viktor said.

"Okay, come on board," Dmitry replied. "Do you have the girl?"

"Yes."

Tony jabbed his gun into Viktor's back also to ensure that he didn't get any wise ideas about telling them who else was with them. As they neared the yacht, Jonathan noticed the black EC155 helicopter on the helipad. He turned to

Jennifer and whispered. "The deal is going down right now," he said in a low tone as they walked slightly behind the group.

"How do you know?"

"The chopper. That one belongs to the Sheik. Jenkins and Steiner told us about that one. They said it would be here if it wasn't too late," Jonathan said, trying to keep his voice down as much as possible.

"What are we going to do?" Jennifer asked, also whispering.

"Put in your earpiece and play it by ear, but stay close to me," he said.

"Okay," she replied. She reached over and gave his hand a quick squeeze. He could see the nervousness on her face. She had been through such a tremendous ordeal, and it was unnerving for him to watch her continue to endure the stress of the entire situation. He wanted it to be over. He wanted the whole thing just to be over.

"It's going to be okay. I promise. I won't let anything happen to you," Jonathan whispered, as they walked across a gravel parking lot that led to the docks. They made their way up the platform and through the security gate that Viktor opened with a key fob.

Don Cicerone looked back to ensure that the entire

group was still with him. He saw Jonathan and Jennifer trailing close behind and motioned with his head for them to quicken their pace. Jonathan looked up at the deckhands that awaited the group and could hear them calling something out. The group continued ascending the platform onto the yacht until they were all on board.

Once on board, one of the deckhands led them to the upper deck of the vessel where the group was still seated for the exchange of the list. When Boris saw them, he pushed his chair back, stood up, and started screaming something in Russian. Viktor looked down at the ground as the Sheik's two personal bodyguards also quickly stood up from the table and brandished their own weapons. Dmitry pulled a gun as well and everyone stood there frozen solid with guns in the air. Jonathan glanced nervously at the two laptops on the table and hoped they weren't too late.

"Wait, please. Please, just wait," Jonathan said. He looked anxiously at Jennifer. What had they done? He stepped forward in front of the group to try to calm everyone's frayed nerves before they started firing. He purposefully stepped in front of Jennifer so that she would be out of harm's way. "Look, no one has to get hurt here. Please, just hear me out," he said.

"Shut up, kid," said Don Cicerone, moving him aside,

back next to Jennifer. "This isn't the time or the place for you to be a tough guy. Let me handle this," he added.

"Okay, but we're outnumbered," Jonathan said. But they weren't outnumbered, and Jonathan knew that. He was just playing coy; he needed to distract them while they could break off from the group before everyone started shooting each other.

A quarter mile away, at the far side of the dock, atop a building, two snipers setup their .308 caliber rifles at the bridge of a roof in clear shot of the upper deck to the yacht. They were adorned in all black garbs, and were in radio communications with Agents Jenkins and Steiner who were organizing the grand takedown.

"Let me know when you guys have locked in on the targets," said Jenkins over the radio.

"Target in sight," said the first sniper.

"Target in plain sight," said the second sniper.

They were aiming at the Sheik's bodyguards who still stood brandishing their weapons in front of the Sheik, who was now just cowering behind them. Beneath all of his wealth and his self-professed dangerous ways, he was just a scared man who had to hide behind the guise of others.

During the concoction of their plan, Jonathan and Jennifer were given small ear implants, which allowed them to stay in two-way communication with the agents, in order to let them know what was going on from their end. Jonathan and Jennifer both overheard all the chatter and could hear that the snipers had taken aim at the Sheik's bodyguards. They breathed a little bit easier knowing that help was secured but hidden, but they still had to grapple with ensuring that things went smoothly. The pair looked at one another as the snipers spoke. They could hear them, and they knew that the shots were about to be fired. Then, they turned their attention to the Don, who was barking orders and aiming his gun at Boris.

"I think you know why I'm here, Medviek," said Don Cicerone. Vinnie and Tony were also pointing their guns at Medviek, who had his own gunmen trained on the group. "I want the cipher drive, and I want it now. It belongs to me," he barked, while holding the gun steady at Medviek's head and grabbing Viktor by the neck.

"Boss, I'm sorry. I'm…" Viktor was pleading with Medviek to forgive him, but there was no way out. He brought trouble to the boat and he brought it in a big way. But, what Boris didn't realize was that sniper rifles were trained on the upper deck, just waiting for the word to take the shot. Both Jennifer and Jonathan knew the word they would say in order to initiate the order. It was part of the plan they had concocted with the Agents.

"Everyone please, just hold on a second. Let's just all put the guns down," Jonathan said. "Let's talk this out. Let's figure this out. Nobody has to get hurt," Jonathan said. He was just trying to distract everyone. He was trying to make cooler heads prevail but nobody was biting. He knew that was a lie, because someone was most certainly going to get hurt. He looked in Jennifer's eyes and she knew what he was thinking, but with all the guns trained on one another, it was too risky.

"Nobody has to get hurt?" Boris asked. He started laughing uncontrollably. "Nobody has to get hurt? Who the hell do you think you are?"

"Honestly, nobody. I'm just doing my job. That's all."

"Your job?" Boris walked closer to him, his gun trained on Jonathan's head, while the three Italians kept their guns pointed at Medviek. He didn't seem to flinch at the fact that everyone was pointing guns at everyone else. He still felt like he was invincible. He felt like nothing could hurt him.

"Yes, just my job," Jonathan said silently.

"And what is your job silly little man?" Boris gave out a sinister laugh as he waved his gun around. Everyone followed the gun with their eyes, as if at any moment everyone was going to start shooting.

Jonathan observed the tattoo alongside Boris's neck. It was of an old symbol for Soviet Russia. He could see it in all its detail as Medviek walked closer to him. Jonathan was almost staring down the barrel of the Russian's gun. He started stepping away as Boris stepped closer, guns still following one another.

"Hold it right there," Don Cicerone said. "Listen to me you piece of Russian trash. This has nothing to do with him. The problem you have is with me, and if I don't get my cipher drive back right now, everyone on this boat is going to eat it, including you."

He stopped dead in his tracks, and turned to look at the Don. "Oh yeah?" Boris asked. Now he walked towards Don Cicerone, who was still holding Viktor tightly by the neck, creating a barrier in front of him. It didn't stop Boris from keeping his gun trained directly at Viktor who was standing in the way.

"I should just shoot you right now," Don Cicerone said.

"Go ahead, make my day, as you all say in your Hollywood movies," Boris said, mocking the group. "You're on my boat. You don't tell me what to do. I tell you what to do. You think you can just come on here and muscle me around. You have another thing coming if you think that," he barked.

After Boris was finished barking at the Don, four of Medviek's goons had appeared who now had the group surrounded. Jonathan had put his gun in his waist, but as he eyed Jennifer who could almost read his mind, he decided against reaching for it. He listened to the chatter in his earpiece.

Agent Jenkins: "What's the status?"

Sniper 1: "Suspects have the group surrounded. The Sheik is heading towards the helicopter.

Sniper 2: "I have the shot. Permission to fire?"

Agent Jenkins: "No. It's too risky. We haven't gotten the signal yet. They haven't said the code word."

NSA Director Edwards: "Snipers, you stand down until we give the orders."

Sniper 1: "But, sir?"

NSA Director Edwards: "I said stand down."

Jonathan and Jennifer listened in closely. They knew it was going to be too difficult for them to get the shots off without them getting hurt. They were at odds with what to do. But, then Jonathan got an idea. He looked over at Jennifer as if to tell her to play along. Jonathan stepped back from the group and so did Jennifer.

"Snowball!" yelled Jonathan. Everyone turned and looked at him, but only he and Jennifer knew what that meant.

"Snowball!" yelled Jennifer almost in unison with Jonathan. It was the code word. Everyone looked at one another too confused to understand what was going on. Had they heard them?

"Snowball!" Jonathan yelled it again, and again as he backed away. Boris moved towards Jonathan again this time pointing the gun at him.

Agent Jenkins: "We have the command. Go. Go."

Sniper 2: "I have the shot. Sir?"

Agent Jenkins: "Take out the Sheik's body guards. We can't have him leave."

Sniper 1: "Permission to fire?"

NSA Director Edwards: "Fire. Fire. Permission Granted."

As Jonathan and Jennifer heard the chatter on the earpieces, they dove down to the ground as the shots were fired. Two quick shots took out the Sheik's bodyguards, leaving him stunned. As the shots rang down in front of the helicopter, the pilot quickly powered the chopper's engines and the propellers started spinning. The loud propellers made it difficult to hear anything anyone else was saying.

Boris looked stunned as four more shots rung out and all of the armed deckhands were taken out, and the Italians stood there stunned. In the commotion, Viktor broke away from Don Cicerone and ran towards the railing of the superyacht, jumped atop, and hurled himself off and into the ocean. Don Cicerone, seeing this, pointed his gun towards the water and stared unloading, firing his weapon into the dark blue waters. His two goons kept their guns trained on Medviek, who was now unprotected.

Seeing this, Jonathan knew it was his only chance. He bum-rushed the Russian as Dmitry took out his gun and pointed it towards Jonathan. As he was about to fire, Vinnie and Tony started unloading their weapons into Dmitry. The whole deck sounded like a fireworks parade as blood was spattered everywhere. Jennifer, grasping her still-hurt shoulder, watched as bodies hit the polished wood decking of the superyacht with thuds.

"No! Jonathan!" she yelled at him as he rushed towards the Russian. Jonathan hit him with all the force he could muster up. He slammed Medviek to the ground. Then, he jumped on top of him and they struggled on the deck, punching one another as Boris's gun was kicked to the ground. Jennifer was helpless and all she could do was watch. "No! Please stop!" she yelled. "Please!"

She reached down, grabbed the gun in her hands, and stood up slowly. She looked down at the two of them and yelled one more time: "Stop!" The pair stopped wrestling on the deck and Jonathan broke free and stood up slowly, backing away. Boris started to get up as well and Jennifer yelled at him. "No! You stay right there," she said as she pointed the gun directly at him.

"Jennifer, put the gun down," Jonathan said.

"No, he won't stop coming after us until we're dead. It's either him or us, Jonathan," she said, gritting her teeth. She was seething with anger. All of the stress and the anxiety had all boiled over until it had erupted in a fit of rage, and now she was the one calling the shots. She was the one that was holding the gun and had the power. She was the one who had the option of ending someone's life if she chose to. She was no longer going to be a pawn in someone else's chess game. "I've had it!" she yelled again.

"No!" Jonathan yelled at her as she fired a shot right next to Boris's head. He had spun out of the way just in time and grabbed her leg, sending her to the ground. She screamed and yelled as he pulled at her to get the gun.

"You little bitch!" Boris yelled.

"No!" Jonathan yelled again. This time, the Italians came forward and stood over the Russian, kicking the gun out of his hand just before he had a chance to unload the bullets into Jennifer.

"You stay right there," Don Cicerone said, pointing the gun straight down at him. In the commotion, the Sheik had jumped into the helicopter just as it was taking off, and the group turned their attention to the chopper as it whirred to life, sending wind whipping across the entire upper deck.

Jonathan and Jennifer listened into the chatter on their earpieces as more commands were being yelled into their ears.

NSA Director Edwards: "Does he have the laptop? Does the Sheik have the laptop?" he asked in a hastened manner.

Sniper 1: "I have a shot. Should I take out the bird?"

Jonathan: "He does not have the laptop. Repeat. He does not have the laptop. Laptop is secure."

NSA Director Edwards: "Snipers, stand down. I repeat. Stand down. We don't want to cause an international incident."

Sniper 1: "Yes sir."

Sniper 2: "Yes sir. Understood."

The EC155 chopper lifted off the deck of the superyacht and made a thunderous noise as it turned and hovered away from the boat, disappearing into the distant horizon. The Sheik was gone, but the list was safe. And, as Boris lay on the ground, the Italians approached him closely, ready to unload their weapons when Agent Jenkins and Steiner showed up and told everyone to put their guns down.

"Put your guns down. Everyone. Now," Jenkins said forcefully.

"Now, people." Steiner reiterated the call to put down their weapons.

As the Italians turned their backs on Boris, he took his one and only chance to run. He bolted from the deck and into the depths of the yacht, quietly disappearing out of sight.

"You let him get away," Don Cicerone said to them.

"He's not going anywhere. Don't worry," Agent Steiner said. "There's nowhere he can run." They followed Boris down to the lower level and into the bowels of the vessel. He had gone missing. They left the group out on the upper deck and it was pure carnage. There were bodies everywhere.

Jonathan got up and walked over to Jennifer. "Are you okay?"

"Yes, I think so," she said.

Jonathan reached down, grabbed her by her good arm, and lifted her up. "That was scary," he said.

"Tell me about it," she replied. "Oh my god, Jonathan,

Boris still has the cipher drive. We have to follow him."

"You mean this cipher drive?" he said, pulling out both cipher drives from his pocket.

"But? Wait… how did you? I don't get it…" Jennifer was confused. Somehow, Jonathan had retrieved the cipher drive and was holding both of them in his hand.

"On the ground, when we were wrestling together, I managed to slip it out of his pocket," he said, smiling. "That's why I bum-rushed him. He probably thinks he still has it with him."

"How did you…How did you do that?" she asked as they walked off towards the stern of the yacht.

"Impressed?" he asked.

"Yeah, just a little," she said smiling at him. He threw his arms around her waist and pulled her in closer for a kiss. His lips melted as he felt the electricity of her body near his.

Jonathan pulled back and looked into Jennifer's eyes. "Hey, we're not out of the water yet," he said. They could hear commotion coming from one of the lower decks. They could hear yelling and screaming. Jonathan could hear people running across the superyacht, even from up there.

"What's going on down there?" Jennifer asked. Jonathan could see the fear in her eyes again.

"I don't know, but we should go see," he said.

25

Boris had made his way to the lower level in an attempt to board a speedboat, which was anchored to the side of the yacht, but the two agents had him cornered. Jonathan and Jennifer appeared just in time to see all of the commotion and yelling. They saw Boris run behind a pillar. Jenkins barked at them to stay back. Just as Jenkins was yelling at them, Boris fired two shots, just narrowly missing Jonathan and Jennifer, but the slug traveled until it hit Steiner in the chest who had just rounded the corner and was running towards the Russian.

"No!" Jenkins yelled. "Get down!" She tried to call to Steiner but it was too late. He had already been hit and had fallen on the deck of the boat in a pool of blood. Jenkins cursed and stood up discharging her weapon as she moved towards Medviek. "You bastard!" she yelled as she unloaded the weapon, hitting Boris in the shoulder, the arm, and the leg.

"Stand down! Stand down!" NSA Director Edwards could be heard barking orders over the earpiece.

But the shots were too little too late. He was running. Boris had made his escape, running across the dock, and tumbling over the railing and into the awaiting speedboat, which roared its engines as it kicked up enormous amounts of water, spun around, and sped off. He was gone. Before anyone could say or do anything else, he had disappeared.

"He's getting away!" yelled Jonathan, but it was too late. Jenkins was weeping as Steiner gasped for air.

"That bastard," she said, between tears. Jonathan and Jennifer walked over to her and tried to console her.

"I'm so sorry," Jennifer said. She kneeled down and placed her hand on his head. "I'm so, so sorry."

But, Steiner gasped for air and spit up blood. He tilted his head to the side and he was still breathing. "Oh my God! Oh my God! He's alive! Steiner? Steiner, are you with me?" Jenkins asked.

Steiner looked her in the eyes and cracked a half smile, and Jenkins burst into further tears. "You're alive. I thought you were dead."

Jonathan looked over at Steiner lying there. "Hang in there. You're going to be okay. Just hang in there," he said.

"Someone call an ambulance!" Jennifer yelled.

"You're going to be okay, Steiner. You're going to be okay," Jenkins said. As an ambulance arrived and left with Steiner, Jenkins stood with Jonathan and Jennifer.

"I can't thank you enough," Jonathan said.

"I'm just happy we made it out in one piece," Jenkins said. "I was just doing my job."

"Is he going to be okay?" Jennifer asked.

"Yeah, I think he's going to be fine. He's going to have some battle wounds, but he'll recover," Jenkins said.

Jennifer looked at her and gave her a big hug. "Now what?" Jennifer asked.

"Now, we destroy this cipher drive," Jenkins said.

"We do?" Jennifer asked.

"Yes, we do," Jonathan, said.

"You do have the cipher drive, right?" Jenkins asked.

"Yes, it's right here," Jonathan said. He pulled out the replica cipher drive from his pocket, its chrome edge glistening in the sunlight.

"I'll take that," Jenkins said, holding out her hands.

"Here you go. Happy to be rid of this thing once and for all," Jonathan said.

"Me too," said Jennifer. "Me too…"

*****

"Kid, you did good," said Don Cicerone back at the hotel in Taksim Square.

Jonathan handed him the real cipher drive. "I think this belongs to you," he said.

Don Cicerone looked at the cipher drive in his hand, and then he closed his pudgy fingers around it. "Yes. It most certainly does."

"And how about our deal?" Jonathan asked. They were all seated in the lobby of the hotel, which was awash with sunlight.

"Our deal?" asked the Don, who smiled at Jonathan.

"Yeah. Our deal." he looked at Jennifer with uneasiness. She could just see her telling him *I told you so*.

"Oh I'm just pulling your leg kid. Vinnie, give him the briefcase," said the Don.

"Here you go," Vinnie barked in his deep Italian tone. "Here it is." He pushed over the black leather briefcase and Jonathan slid it onto his lap and held it there. He unclicked the two locks and opened it up, peeking inside. His eyes widened as he saw the stacks of hundred dollar bills that lined the interior.

"It was a pleasure," said the Don.

Jonathan smiled back, quickly closed the briefcase, and locked it back up. "Pleasure was all mine," Jonathan cooed as he reeled from the shock of having nearly a million dollars in his hands.

"What's next for you two?" the Don asked, looking directly at Jennifer this time.

"Wherever the day takes us," she said, reaching over to grab Jonathan's hand.

"Hey, look at these two lovebirds," Tony said. He chuckled and all the Italians laughed along with him.

THANK YOU

Don't Forget to Leave a Review

I sincerely hope that you enjoyed reading this story just as much as I enjoyed writing it. I would appreciate it if you could take a few moments out of your day to leave a review on Amazon by clicking the following link: http://www.amazon.com/dp/B00EJSXYV6

Thank you.

All the Best,
Robert Stohn

Printed in Great Britain
by Amazon